'Well?' Jackson said softly, too softly, instinct warned her.

Trembling, Chrissie pushed herself up straighter in the chair and tried to answer, but it was difficult to think under the force of that hostile, obsidian gaze.

'Cat got your tongue, then?' he asked gently, and a sudden colour flared under her skin at his mocking tone. He knew she was terrified, knew she was almost struck dumb by fear, and he was enjoying it . . . damn him! There was no way she was going to afford him even one moment more of pleasure. Anger spurted through her, unlocking her tongue.

'I came to see Mr Knight. I have an appointment with him. He's expecting me.' It was the truth, or had been some half-hour ago, and she clung to it like a drowning man to a shaky raft.

'Oh, he is, is he? I see. And do you always come in the back way for appointments, and creep through the place like a thief?'

A MAGICAL TOUCH

BY

JENNIFER TAYLOR

MILLS & BOON LIMITED
ETON HOUSE   18-24 PARADISE ROAD
RICHMOND   SURREY   TW9 1SR

First published in Great Britain 1989
by Mills & Boon Limited

© *Jennifer Taylor 1989*

Australian copyright 1989
Philippine copyright 1989
This edition 1989

ISBN 0 263 76476 1

Set in English Times 11 on 11½ pt.
01 – 8911 – 49263

Typeset in Great Britain by JCL Graphics, Bristol

Made and Printed in Great Britain

CHAPTER ONE

LATE, late, for a very important date!

The words wove a pattern round her brain as fast as her feet wove a path through the crowds blocking the pavement. Flicking a glance at her watch, Chrissie bit back a groan as she realised she was nearly twenty minutes late for the appointment. Would he understand, accept her excuse that the bus had gone early and left her stranded? Or would he refuse to see her? She'd have to wait and see, but if she'd blown it, her one chance, then she would never forgive herself.

She raced up the shallow flight of steps into the club, and stared round the huge, empty hallway, taking rapid stock of the rich ruby-red carpet, the enormous chandeliers, the heavily ornate antique furniture, and felt her insides tighten in sudden revulsion. The whole place screamed money, and lots of it, but the question was, how had it been come by? If what she suspected was right, then by the worst, most despicable way possible.

'Yes? May I help you?'

The cool, faintly hostile voice startled her, and Chrissie swung round, her eyes racing to the woman standing behind her, one darkly perfect eyebrow raised in enquiry.

'I . . . I've an appointment to see Mr Knight at eleven,' she stammered, her tongue tripping in nervous haste. 'I'm sorry I'm late, but I missed the bus and had to wait ages for another to come along.'

'I see.'

Unsmiling, the woman let her eyes drift over Chrissie from head to toe, a trace of distaste on her beautifully made-up features, and instinctively Chrissie stood up a touch straighter. She was a mess and she knew it, the hasty race across town having played havoc both with her appearance and her composure, but there was no way she was going to let this woman look down her nose at her! She pushed back a long, silky strand of blonde hair which had come free from its clasp and faced her squarely, a touch of steel to her usually quiet tones when she spoke.

'As I don't wish to be even later than I am already, would you mind checking if Mr Knight can see me? The name is Lane, Christina Lane. My agent, Joe Parker, made the appointment for the audition.'

The woman nodded, her face still cold. 'Yes, I know. I'm Moira Wade, Mr Knight's personal assistant. However, I'm afraid that Mr Knight can't see you now. He's already auditioning someone else.'

Little apology tinged her voice and, looking at her, Chrissie had the sudden, irrational feeling that she was deriving some sort of pleasure from the situation, though why she couldn't imagine. Not that it mattered, of course, not that anything mattered except the fact that she had to see Jackson Knight. It was absolutely vital that she got this job . . . she owed it to Kate.

Tears sprang to her eyes at the thought of her sister and she quickly blinked them away, knowing she couldn't afford to weaken at the moment. She had to convince this woman to let her see him, somehow.

'Surely he can fit me in later? Look, Miss Wade, I don't care how long I have to wait till he's free, so please won't you ask him?' Sheer desperation added a touch of entreaty to her voice, but it was lost on the brunette.

'I'm sorry, but that's quite impossible. All I can suggest is that you get your agent to make another appointment. Mr Knight is a very busy man and he has a full schedule for the rest of the day. There's no way it can be altered to accommodate latecomers.'

And no way you'd even try, Chrissie thought with a sudden flash of bitter insight. But she couldn't just leave without making every effort possible to get in to see Knight. While it stuck in her throat to beg, she'd do it . . . for Kate.

'Oh, please, couldn't you . . .'

'I'm sorry. As I said, it's really quite impossible. Now, if you will excuse me, we are very busy at the moment.'

She crossed the hall to hold the door open, mocking scorn on her face, and Chrissie knew there was no point in trying to pursue it. Snatching up the case she'd brought with her, she strode out of the door, her temper flaring as she heard the sound of a bolt being shot behind her. Just who did that woman think she was? What did she think

Chrissie was going to do . . . sneak back in and see Jackson Knight without her permission?

The thought spun into her mind, stopping her short. Could she do it, find some way back into the club and see him? What if it all went wrong? Surely then she would only be making a bad situation worse? Perhaps it would be more sensible to wait, to make another appointment . . . if she could! Suddenly Chrissie had a deep-seated and totally inexplicable feeling that making another appointment mightn't be as easy as it sounded: Moira Wade would see to that! No, she couldn't afford to wait, to miss this chance when there might never be another one.

Fired with renewed determination, she made her way quickly round to the back of the building and peered round the heavy wooden gates which enclosed the rear courtyard, trying to find a way inside. It didn't really matter what it was: an open window, a fire-escape, even a cat-flap! Frankly, she didn't have the time to be choosy.

The back door was open. For a few, interminable seconds Chrissie stood and stared at the tantalising opening, her heart racing with a sudden fear. It was such an awful risk, but could she manage to sneak in now while the door was open? It might be the only chance she would get, so really it was just too good to miss.

Clamping the case to her side, she hurried across the yard, her eyes flicking nervously from side to side, praying there was no one watching. Suddenly a movement at one of the windows on the first floor caught her attention and she froze. Was someone there, standing behind that tinted glass, watching her? Or had it just been a shadow, a flicker of sunlight? Shading her eyes against the glare, she stared at the window, but no matter how hard she tried she couldn't see any further sign of movement, and with a tiny shrug she hurried on, wondering if she'd imagined it.

The back door led directly into a large store-room and Chrissie hesitated, trying to get her bearings. From somewhere deeper inside the building came the soft murmur of voices, and she knew she couldn't afford to linger. At any moment someone could come along and find her. She had to get out of this room, make her way through to where the auditions were being held, then she would only have to convince Knight to see her and she was home and dry. Simple . . . like hell!

As quickly as possible she made her way from the room and along the corridors, only pausing when she arrived at a small, square hallway, its floor covered in the same red carpet she'd seen earlier. It was obvious from the décor that she'd now passed into the main part of the club, yet she was still no wiser as to where to find Jackson Knight. What should she do?

Undecided, she stared round and then she heard it, the faint but unmistakable sound of music playing and a woman singing, very badly and distinctly off-key, but the sweetest sound she'd heard in ages: the sound of someone auditioning! But where was it coming from?

For several minutes she stood quite still, trying to pinpoint the direction of the sound. It appeared to be coming from behind the door opposite, yet because the wood was so thick it was impossible to be absolutely certain. The auditions might be taking place on the other side of that door, or they might not, but the only way she could tell exactly was to open it and see. Heaven alone knew what she might find on the other side, but it was a chance she would just have to take. She'd come too far now to turn back.

She drew in a deep, steadying breath, then eased the door open just far enough to squeeze both herself and the case inside, stopping abruptly when her eyes encountered an inky darkness. The singing was louder now, the music throbbing and pulsing through the air, and, faintly reassured, she moved further into the room, letting the door close behind her. She stood quite still, straining to see through the darkness.

The music stopped, so suddenly that Chrissie caught her breath in surprise, feeling her heart start to hammer wildly as silence closed round her like a crushing hand. Everywhere was so still, so utterly quiet now, no glimmer of light or whisper of sound issuing from any direction, yet suddenly, somehow, she knew she wasn't alone. There was someone there, someone sharing that darkness with her. She couldn't explain what sixth sense told her, she just knew, and terror crawled like icy fingers up her spine. She had to get out, had to get away from whatever was waiting in the room!

She dropped the case and swung round, strangely disorientated by the darkness so that for a moment she couldn't remember in which direction the door lay. She raised her hands, feeling blindly in front of her for its smooth wooden surface, and froze as her searching fingers brushed against the unmistakable hardness of another body.

'What took you so long? I've been waiting.'

The voice was low, deeply masculine and filled with so much quiet menace that Chrissie threw all caution to the winds. She screamed, just as long and as hard as she could!

'What the he——'

The oath was bitten off and lights flared with a blinding suddenness, damming the screams in her throat. Chrissie raised her hands, shielding her eyes against the vicious glare, her whole body trembling in reaction.

'Sit down.'

Strong hands caught her roughly by the shoulders, pushing her down into a chair and, leaning back, she tried to contain the weakness which threatened to claim her. She breathed deeply, forcing oxygen into her lungs, then slowly looked up into the coldest, hardest black eyes she had ever seen, and shivered.

There was a moment's pause, a split second of silence while she and the man stared at each other, then a harsh rapping at the door broke the spell.

'What's happening in there? What's going on?'

The gruff demand was accompanied by another even louder pounding on the solid wood, and with a low curse the man swung away to fling it open.

'For pity's sake, Thompson, you'll have it off its hinges if you carry on like that!'

'Sorry, but I heard someone screaming and didn't know if you needed help,' the man outside answered, sounding suddenly uncertain. He peered into the room, staring at Chrissie with an avid curiosity, but frankly she still felt too shocked to care what anyone was thinking!

'Well, it sure as hell wasn't me who screamed, so get back to work. I'll call you if and when I need you.'

He slammed the door, then turned, and Chrissie felt herself blanch at the hostile expression on his face. She swallowed hard, desperately trying to find her voice, to find something to say which could ease the tension which filled the room, but it was hopeless. Her mouth was dry as old leather, her tongue still thick with lingering terror, making it impossible to speak. Dumbly she watched as he came back towards her and stopped just a few feet away, his dark eyes pinned to her face.

'Well?' he said softly, too softly, instinct warned her.

Trembling, she pushed herself up straighter in the chair and tried to answer, but it was difficult to think under the force of that hostile, obsidian gaze.

'Cat got your tongue, then?' he asked gently, and a sudden colour flared under her skin at his mocking tone. He knew she was terrified, knew she was almost struck dumb by fear, and he was enjoying it . . . damn him! There was no way she was going to afford him even one moment more of pleasure. Anger spurted through her, unlocking her tongue.

'I came to see Mr Knight. I have an appointment

with him. He's expecting me.' It was the truth, or
had been some half-hour ago, and she clung to it
like a drowning man to a shaky raft.

'Oh, he is, is he? I see. And do you always come
in the back way for appointments, and creep
through the place like a thief?'

'Of course not,' she retorted hotly, 'I just
happened to spot the back entrance, so I thought
I'd use it to save time. I didn't go "creeping"
anywhere, as you put it.'

'No?' One dark eyebrow rose in mockery as he
watched her, his arms folded across his chest, and
she eyed him warily. Although he wasn't
exceptionally tall, not more than an inch or two
over her own generous five foot ten, he was
strongly built, with wide, powerful shoulders and a
broad, muscular chest tapering down to a narrow,
masculine waist and strong thighs. She had no idea
who he could be, but there was no way that
physique had been gained sitting behind a desk,
pushing a pen, and for a moment she tried to work
out who he was.

Her eyes slid back up over the old, washed jeans
and grey sweatshirt he was wearing to his face and
halted, studying the harsh terrain of plains and
shadows, the slightly overlong, jet-black hair, the
cold black eyes, and in a sudden flash of
inspiration she wondered if he could be one of the
security staff the club was bound to employ. It
seemed likely, more than likely from the look of
him, but if he was then she would have to be very
careful how she acted. In his job, he would
naturally be very suspicious of everything she said.

She had to find some way to convince him that her entry into the club had been just as innocent as she'd tried to make it appear, but how? Perhaps a little feminine charm would oil the way.

She sat up straighter, raising her hand to slowly push the tumble of silky blonde hair away from her face, and hid a smile as she noted his typically male reaction, the way the dark gaze followed her movements to linger appreciatively on the gleaming golden strands. Well, so far, so good; a touch more and, frankly, she'd have him eating out of her hand!

Lips curved into a fetching smile, she stared up at him, her blue eyes as wide and innocent as she could make them.

'Of course I didn't creep in. I just came in the back and walked through. After all, I've absolutely nothing to hide, just a very valid reason to be here.'

Her voice was low, softly gentle, and for a moment he stared down at her, his dark eyes lingering on her parted lips.

'I see.'

He turned abruptly away and, puzzled, Chrissie watched him, wondering what he was up to . . . but not for long. He reached up to flick a row of switches, and a line of screens set high into the wall sprang into life, each one framing a different view of the interior of the building. Staring at the flickering grey images, Chrissie had no difficulty picking out the store-room and the back hall, and her blood turned to sudden, freezing ice as she grasped the implications.

'You saw me,' she croaked out through strangely

numb lips, and he nodded, a grimly satisfied smile curving his mouth.

'Right from the first moment you peered round the yard door. That beautiful face and hair might be enough to get you out of most things, lady, but it was what made me notice you in the first place. After all, how many gorgeous blondes do you find skulking round back alleys, unless they're up to something—well, how shall I put it, not quite legal?'

There was a barrel of double meanings to his mocking words, and Chrissie felt her damped-down temper flare to life. How dared he? How dared he imply that not only was she here for some nefarious reason, but that she made a habit of skulking round alleys to ply her trade? She stood up, her fists clenched at her sides, and glared hotly at him, her face filled with a righteous indignation.

'Now you listen here, I'm not in the habit of skulking round anywhere, for your information. OK, so maybe I did take a back route in to find Mr Knight, but that's only because I was desperate to see him.'

'And you just happened to end up in here, in this room?' he said flatly.

'Well, yes. I heard singing and thought maybe this was where the auditions were being held. Why, what's so special about here?'

She stared round, her eyes skimming over the cream-painted walls to halt abruptly on the metal safe sunk into the one opposite, and her mind did a quantum leap towards understanding, then hopped swiftly backwards in rejection. Surely he didn't believe she'd come in here for that, did he? Why, it was plainly ridiculous. Did she really look like a safebreaker? The man was mad!

'Now, look here——' she started hotly but stopped as he stepped forwards, his face set into grim lines.

'No, you look here, lady. Three times in the past few months we've had attempted break-ins, and on two of those occasions it was reported that a tall blonde had been seen in the area.'

'But that wasn't me. I've never even been here before today!' she cried, suddenly desperate to convince him. He was watching her with an expression in those dark eyes which was frankly scary, and all at once she became aware of just how quiet the building was. If he chose not to believe her, chose to make her admit, by force if need be, to something she'd never done, then she wouldn't stand a chance. She had to convince him of her innocence somehow.

'Listen, please, you must listen to me. I really did have an appointment with Mr Knight, but I was late and he couldn't see me. Ask him . . . please.'

The man studied her quietly for a second, then walked slowly to the huge mahogany desk and sat down on the very edge of it, his eyes never leaving her face. Suddenly Chrissie knew he wasn't going to do as she'd just begged him. He didn't believe her, didn't believe one single word she'd told him, and there was no way he ever would. She looked round, desperately trying to think, to find a way out of the situation, but it was hopeless. In a sudden flash she realised there was only one option open to her: she had to get away, and fast!

She spun round, raced across the room to the door and turned the handle, twisting it first one way then another when it refused to give under her frantic hands.

'It's locked.'

The low, flat statement halted her movements, and slowly she let her hands fall to her sides in despair, before staring across the width of the room at her tormentor.

'Why?' she cried. 'Why won't you believe me? Why won't you find Mr Knight and ask him, get him to check his appointments? He'll confirm I'm telling the truth.'

'Why?' he repeated softly, pushing away from the desk to cross the room and stop just inches from her. 'Well, I'll tell you why, seeing as you've asked. Because I am Jackson Knight, that's why.'

Dumb with shock and confusion, Chrissie stared back at him for several seconds, till slowly it came to her that not only had she lost her one chance, but the whole damned game! Now she would never be able to help Kate, and the tears she'd held in check all these long, dreadful weeks spilled over to run down her cheeks in a silvery tide.

CHAPTER TWO

CHRISSIE cried for several minutes—deep, silent sobs which racked her slender frame as the enormity of it all hit her—and he just watched her, saying nothing. Then, when the tears started to abate, he turned away, strode across the room to the desk and punched a button on the small intercom system.

'Yes, Mr Knight.'

The voice which answered was faint, but Chrissie had no difficulty identifying its cool tones as those of his assistant, Moira Wade, even through the last, lingering waves of her despair.

'Come in, please, Moira.'

'Now? But, Mr Knight . . .'

'Now.' His tone brooked no argument as he cut the connection and straightened, his dark eyes skimming over Chrissie, who was still huddled where he'd left her against the door.

'Why don't you sit down?' he asked quietly, and she stiffened, feeling in the pocket of her jacket for a tissue to wipe her face before she answered with as much dignity as she could muster.

'What for? So you can accuse me of something else . . . think up some more fanciful lies about me?'

Her voice was harshly bitter, and just for a moment she wondered if she'd struck a chord as he looked away, a strange, fleeting expression on his face—but then again, just who was she kidding? This man, who incredibly had turned out to be Jackson Knight, was pure granite right through to the very core; there was no way anything she said could possibly get to him. Clamping her lips together, she stared mutinously at him across the width of the room, an icy disdain showing in her eyes. Heaven knew, she'd never expected to like him, but nothing had prepared her for this feeling of animosity which filled her.

There was a brief silence, then he spoke, his voice cool and level, revealing nothing of what he was feeling.

'I just thought you'd be better off sitting down before you fell down, but if you'd rather stand, then please yourself.'

He pulled out the high-backed leather chair behind the desk and sat down, and instantly Chrissie regretted her hasty refusal. She did feel shaky, her legs trembling with the aftermath of all she'd gone through this past half-hour, but there was no way she was going to give him even the tiniest morsel of satisfaction by admitting it now. She would rather suffer!

She shoved the crumpled tissue back into her pocket, then pushed her hair away from her hot face. Most of it seemed to have escaped from the tortoiseshell clasp she'd caught it back with that morning, and with a quick flick she pulled the rest free, letting the soft, silky waves cascade round her shoulders in a golden cloud.

'Is it naturally that colour?'

Comfortably settled in the chair, Knight was watching her, his dark eyes riveted to her hair as though he'd never seen anything like it before. Chrissie nodded, then looked away, disconcerted by his obvious interest, feeling the colour flood up her face in a warm tide. He laughed, a low ripple of sound, and she stiffened, shooting a swift glance in his direction, her pulse racing as she caught his eyes.

'It's incredible, really,' he said softly, his dark eyes holding hers. 'A thief who blushes . . . no one's ever going to believe it when I tell them.'

His tone was frankly insulting, and Chrissie flinched, anger starting to burn inside her and chase away the chills of disappointment and terror. She was no thief, and there was no way she was going to stand there and let him call her one. Eyes blazing, she glared at him, about to tell him exactly what she thought of him and his foul insinuations, when a soft knock came at the door and she hesitated. The handle turned, then was rattled when the door failed to open.

'Mr Knight . . . are you in there?'

'Just a moment.'

He stood up to open the door, and instinctively Chrissie stepped aside to let him pass, moving further into the room to stand by the desk, her hand unconsciously seeking its support. She had no idea what he was up to, but if his previous record was anything to go by, then it seemed more than likely that it would be nothing pleasant! She watched as he swung the door open to let Moira Wade enter, a strangely intent look on his face as he studied her reaction—and it was worth studying, that was certain.

Shock, surprise, then cold fury crossed her perfect features in swift succession when she spotted Chrissie standing by the desk.

'What are you doing here?' she demanded abruptly.

Then she swung round, her face paling as Knight said with a deceptive mildness, 'It appears you know our "visitor", then, Moira.'

There was something in his voice, something which Chrissie couldn't quite identify, but which made the back of her neck prickle, and in a sudden rush she realised that so far she'd been very lucky: so far Jackson Knight had afforded her kid-glove treatment, if that tone was anything to go by. There was a ruthlessness to the man, an innate hardness which warned her he'd be capable of anything, even the dreadful thing she suspected. But he would pay for what he'd done, to Kate and all those others. She would see to that, if she could just get this job!

'Well, Moira?'

He sat down behind the desk again, his face unreadable.

'I . . . yes, Mr Knight. I met Miss Lane earlier.' With an almighty effort Moira Wade finally answered, her eyes sliding over Chrissie with venom in their pale depths.

'I see, and where was that?'

His tone was icily cold and clear, and Chrissie shivered, glad that she wasn't on the receiving end of this inquisition.

'In the front hall, about half an hour ago.'

'And did you find out what she was doing there?' he asked steadily, his dark eyes never leaving the woman's face.

'Yes, of course. She had an appointment for an audition at eleven, but as she was so late in arriving, I knew it would be impossible to fit her in just then, so I suggested that she wait till later.'

It was such a blatant lie that Chrissie gasped, her eyes racing from Knight to the woman.

'You did no such thing! I asked if I could wait to see Mr Knight later, but you said there was no point as he would be tied up for the rest of the day. Why, I would never have gone through all this charade if you'd told me I could wait!' Indignation added a flush to her cheeks, a flush which deepened as she realised that Jackson Knight had turned his attention to her now.

'Oh, no, Miss Lane. You must have misunderstood me. I distinctly remember saying that you could wait, if you wanted to.'

Why was she lying? Chrissie couldn't fathom the reason for it, unless it was to escape the full force of Jackson Knight's anger—and that she could appreciate. One didn't need a degree in psychology to know that he would take a very dim view of an employee's making a decision without consulting him first.

The realisation kept Chrissie quiet, though annoyance flared through her as she noticed the fleeting expression of satisfaction on Moira's face at her silence. It didn't take much to know that, if the situation had been reversed, Moira Wade would never have worried about getting Chrissie into trouble!

'So it appears there has been some sort of misunderstanding, then, doesn't it?' His voice was low but strangely commanding, so that both women focused their attention on him. 'You, Moira, are absolutely certain that—Miss Lane, is it?—had an appointment to see me, are you?'

'Yes, I made it myself when her agent phoned last week,' the brunette replied with a marked reluctance, and Chrissie felt quite certain that she would have given anything to deny it!

'I see. And you, Miss Lane, you still maintain that the only reason you came in the back way was to keep that appointment?'

He stared up at her, one thick, dark eyebrow raised in enquiry, and Chrissie nodded, not trusting herself to speak in case she upset the proceedings. A tiny ray of hope was starting to glow inside her, a hope that maybe things would turn out as she'd planned, after all. Clamping her lips tightly together, she waited to hear what he would say next. So much depended on his decision—so much that she was almost frightened to think about it.

'Right, well, as we seem to have cleared that up, I think you can go now, Moira, but next time please make certain that I am informed of any late arrivals so we can avoid this situation happening again.'

'Yes, Mr Knight,' she replied, her lips tight with annoyance at the rebuke in his tone. 'Shall I see Miss Lane out?' she added quickly, and Chrissie

realised that the woman was most reluctant to leave
her and Knight together. Maybe she was still
worried what Chrissie would say, but she needn't
be. There was no way she was going to upset the
cart now and set all the apples rolling when things
seemed to be starting to go right.

'No, that won't be necessary . . . yet, thank
you,' he said softly. Chrissie shot him a swift
glance, wondering exactly what he meant by that
ambiguous answer. Her eyes traced over his face,
but with the harsh, cold mask which seemed to be
his habitual expression firmly in place it was
impossible to tell what he was thinking. She would
have to wait and see what he came up with . . . pity
help her!

With a marked reluctance Moira left the room,
and there was silence, a silence which seemed to
run on for ever so that Chrissie felt her nerves
stretch to their absolute limits. She shoved her
hands deep into the pockets of her jacket, focused
her gaze on a spot just above Jackson Knight's
dark head, and waited, determined that he would
be the one to break the silence. After all, he was
either going to accept her story now as the truth or
he wasn't; there was little more she could do about
it.

'So it appears I may owe you an apology, after
all.'

His voice was low, but Chrissie still jumped
when he spoke, breaking the silence. She looked
down at him, but there was little in his face that
could be called reassuring. He might be offering
lip-service to an apology, but deep down she had

the feeling he couldn't give a damn whether he'd offended her or not. Jackson Knight wrote and lived by his own code, and if it didn't suit others then it was their hard luck! There was no way he was really going to apologise, to her or anyone. Still, at the moment Chrissie couldn't afford to be choosy; the whole reason she was here was to get the job, and there was no way she could risk antagonising him further. As apologies went, it might be a pitiful example, but she would have to accept it.

Gritting her teeth, she said quickly, 'Well, I'm just glad that we've managed to sort everything out at last.'

'Oh, I wouldn't go as far as to say that, Miss Lane,' he said gently, an underlying thread of steel to his deep voice. 'I still think there's a lot more behind your visit here than you've admitted.'

'What do you mean?'

A sudden fear made her voice shrill and she bit her lip, turning her head slightly so he couldn't read the fast-growing terror in her face. Did he suspect something, have some sort of intuition about her reasons for wanting to work at the club? Could he have recognised her, seen the resemblance between her and Kate? Her mind raced back to how Kate used to look, her skin clear, her red-gold hair cut into a feathery cap which framed her face, her green eyes alight with mischief. Although they were sisters, their colouring was so different that it usually threw people, made them miss the similarity between their delicate features and softly oval-shaped faces, but then, this man wasn't most people. Even though she'd only just met him, Chrissie knew his perception went deeper than other people's. There would be little anyone could hide from Jackson Knight, very little.

The thought made her shiver, her slender body trembling like a leaf on a shaky branch, a movement not missed by the man who was watching her so closely, his dark eyes intent.

'I don't know why exactly, but you seem so nervous, Miss Lane . . . why, I wonder?'

He leant back in his chair, his eyes locked to her pale face, and Chrissie forced herself to meet them, forced down the fear which had started to rise deep inside her. She had to be strong.

'Of course I'm nervous, Mr Knight! Let's face it, one way or another, this has been a very strange morning, so it's little wonder that I seem nervous, is it?'

She forced a lightness to her tone, glad that her hands were still hidden deep in her pockets so that he couldn't see how they trembled, how the nails bit into the soft inner flesh as she curled them into fists. Would he believe her? Holding her breath, she waited to find out.

He shrugged, the massive shoulders moving briefly under his thin sweatshirt. 'I suppose so. As you say, it's been a very strange morning, very strange indeed.'

There was a slight double edge to the words, but Chrissie knew she couldn't afford to let herself dwell on it. She had to make herself believe that she'd fooled him, otherwise she'd never be able to

continue with the deception. Now her main
concern had to be what she'd come for . . . the
audition.

'Well, if you could just tell me where to go to get
changed, then I won't need to waste any more of
your time.'

'Changed?'

'For the audition, Mr Knight. I really can't
perform for you dressed like this.'

She swept a hand down the length of her slender
body to indicate the tight-fitting jeans and sweater
she was wearing under the leather jacket, then
instantly regretted her action when she saw how his
dark eyes followed the movement and lingered in a
look which seemed to burn her flesh like fire.

'No? You look fine to me.'

There was something in his voice, something
which made her pulse leap into sudden, frenzied
action, something which could only be called sheer
seduction, and in a blinding flash she understood
the one thing which had puzzled her all these
weeks: just how Kate could have been held in such
thrall by this man that she'd been prepared to do
anything and risk everything for him! The
realisation was strangely unsettling.

'I suppose I can't stop you if you're really set on
getting changed, but there is just one thing which
you haven't told me yet, Miss Lane.'

His voice broke through her thoughts and she
quickly brought her attention back to the present,
knowing she couldn't afford to be off guard with
him for even a moment.

'What's that, Mr Knight?' she asked as calmly as

she could manage, suddenly wary of what he'd thought of.

'Your act, of course. I haven't any idea what you do. Are you a singer, a dancer, or what?'

He was watching her, a vague look of boredom now on his face, and hastily Chrissie stifled a chuckle of mirth which started to rise inside her at the question. She raised her hands, sliding them gently through her hair, winnowing the long golden strands free from the high collar of her jacket, knowing from past experience just how quickly she could wipe that look off his face with her answer. She took her time, savouring every moment, then smiled at him, her lips tilted into a gentle, mocking curve.

'No, I'm not a singer or a dancer.'

'Then what do you do?' he asked equally softly, his eyes lingering on the golden waves which covered her shoulders.

'What do I do? Why, I'm a magician, Mr Knight,' she said clearly, and watched the shock which rippled through him with a feeling of intense and comforting satisfaction. Abracadabra!

The proverbial pin dropping would have sounded loud as cannon-fire in the silence which followed, a silence which was balm to Chrissie's tortured nerves. It was difficult to remember just how many times she'd gained this effect with her answer to that same question, but it made little difference now to her present enjoyment. Studying the frozen look of surprise on Jackson Knight's face, she knew she would have to go a long way to better his reaction, and the knowledge gave a huge, welcome boost to her confidence. She pulled out the chair and sat down, crossing one long jean-clad leg across the other and waited for all the questions which were bound to follow.

'Did I hear you right? Did you say *magician*?'

To give credit where it was due, he seemed to be recovering faster than many others, but his number one question was still boringly predictable. With a tiny smile she merely nodded, not bothering to waste any breath on a proper answer. She carefully studied her unvarnished oval nails for a second, then buffed them gently against her sweater while she waited for number two.

'Right, then, Miss Lane, I suggest you get changed and show me . . . just how good a magician you really are.'

Her hand froze, her mouth falling open just a fraction in surprise. What was he doing? That wasn't how things usually went! What had happened to all the 'why's and 'how's which always followed that first stunned amazement? She skimmed a glance over his face, just fast enough to catch the fleeting gleam of amusement in his dark eyes before he blanked it out and, with a flash of annoyance, realised he'd understood only too well what she'd been expecting! She snatched up her case and strode towards the door, her face flaming as he said calmly, 'By the way, the dressing-rooms are along the corridor to your left, if you were wondering which way to go.'

There was more than a hint of mockery in his voice and, half turning, Chrissie shot him a look of sheer dislike before striding from the room without

deigning to answer. Resisting the urge to slam the
door behind her, she closed it gently, that dislike
flaring to absolute hatred as she heard the
unmistakable sound of his laughter! Well, he could
laugh all he liked now, but one day, one glorious
day, she'd make him pay . . . for this along with
everything else. Inch by inch and second by second
the score against Mr Insufferable Jackson Knight
was increasing, and she was keeping a careful track
of it!

Twenty soothing minutes later Chrissie stepped
back from the mirror in the small, cramped
dressing-room and viewed herself critically. Her
eyes slid slowly down from the top of her perfectly
arranged blonde hair to the tips of her sequinned
sandals, and she smiled, the tension smoothing
from her face as she realised she'd been right to
choose this outfit. Back at the flat, crammed into
the narrow cupboard which served as a wardrobe,
she had some half-dozen beautiful costumes, most
newly bought for her recent stint at a top Las Vegas
nightclub, but this was her absolute favourite.
Wearing this, she knew she looked her best, and at
the moment she needed that sort of reassurance.

Made from soft, rich, royal-blue satin, the
slender, body-hugging dress made the most of her
slim figure and honey-blonde colouring. Long-
sleeved and high-necked, it appeared almost primly
modest until she moved and the skirt parted to
reveal tantalising glimpses of her long, slender legs
through the thigh-length side splits. With it she
wore ridiculously high silvery sandals, their narrow
four-inch heels adding to her own considerable

height so that she topped the six-foot mark by a couple of inches.

Years ago, when entering her teens, she'd hated being tall and had gone through agonies of embarrassment because of it. Now, however, Chrissie had come to terms with her height and tended to emphasise rather than disguise it, knowing it gave her even more presence when she was up on stage.

With one last, sweeping glance at her reflection, she moved away and quickly gathered up the small collection of items she needed for the audition, packing them carefully into a soft, drawstring bag and murmuring crossly as she fumbled with the tie fastenings. Her hands were shaking and, setting the bag aside, she made herself breathe slowly and deeply in a steady rhythm for several minutes till she could feel the trembling start to abate. After all, the last thing a magician needed was shaking hands!

A light, firm knock sounded at the door, and with a swift glance round to check she had everything she swung it open, her heart leaping when she discovered Jackson Knight standing outside. There was silence while his eyes moved slowly up her body to linger on her face, and she caught her breath as she read the message in their glittering depths.

He wanted her! It was there as clearly as though it had been written, and she shivered, an icy panic uncurling inside her as she saw it. Then, slowly, as they stood silently facing each other, another emotion came to life, a stronger, harsher emotion

which quelled the weakness of panic: anger. Was
this how he'd once looked at Kate? Had he let his
eyes roam over her, too, in this strangely possessive
and intimate way? Had he wanted her like this, or
had he just used her, right from the beginning?

Revulsion flooded through Chrissie at the
thought and she glanced away, terrified he might
see it in her face. The last thing she must do at the
moment was antagonise him, or she would never
get the job. If Jackson Knight found her attractive,
then she should be glad, use it to give her the edge
over any competition . . . if she could. Could she
really handle that sort of complication?

'Ready?' he asked quietly, and Chrissie nodded,
pushing the disturbing idea to the back of her mind
to be dealt with later. Pinning a bright, practised
smile to her lips, she walked past him, a tiny *frisson*
of alarm racing through her when he caught her
arm in a light clasp.

'This way.'

He led her along the corridor, his long, hard
fingers retaining their loose hold, making her flesh
tingle with the contact. She forced herself to walk
calmly with him, forced down the almost
overwhelming urge which rose inside her to pull
away and run as far and as fast as she could from
the club. If she did that, then every single thing
she'd planned on would be ruined, and Kate's last
hope of freedom wiped away.

Thankfully they'd gone no more than a few
yards before he released her to pull open one half
of a set of double doors, and Chrissie hurried
through them, anxious to put as much distance as

she could between herself and this strangely disturbing man. She looked round, her eyes skimming over all the familiar clutter of wires and cables to be found backstage, and felt the tight, nervous tension which gripped her ease a little. This was home ground, territory she understood and a situation she could handle.

'Come this way and I'll introduce you to Mac. He's in charge of all the lighting round here, so I imagine you'll want a word with him before you start.'

He stepped round her and led the way across the back of the stage; Chrissie followed, her eyes focused on his broad back. For a big man he moved easily, lightly, the muscles in his back and shoulders rippling under their thin covering, and for some strange reason she found herself unable to look away. There was something almost hypnotic about the way he moved, about the blatant power of his big body, that drew her gaze.

Totally absorbed in her study of Knight, she failed to see the coil of cable which lay snaked across her path. With startling suddenness, the heel of her sandal caught in the thick wire and she staggered, crying out in alarm as she felt herself falling. Hearing her cry, Knight swung round, his arms reaching out instinctively to catch her as she pitched forwards and cushion her safely against the solid support of his body.

For several seconds Chrissie stayed exactly where she'd landed, her cheek pressed into the hollow of his shoulder, her hands spread across the warm, muscled hardness of his chest so that she could feel the heavy, steady pounding of his heart against her palm. Then slowly the realisation of just who held her flooded through her, and with a tiny gasp of dismay she pulled away. Colour washed up her cheeks and, raising her hands, she made a great show of adjusting a loosened curl while she tried to find some smart, snappy little comment to offer her thanks and dismiss the incident. The trouble was, nothing came to mind!

She felt stunned, totally and utterly stunned, and in a flash of self-honesty admitted that she couldn't lay all the blame on the fall. True, the unexpected speed of it had startled her, but surely it hadn't been enough to set her pulse racing and her heart hammering in this way? Confused and disturbed, Chrissie struggled to find some way to gloss over what had happened, but it was nearly impossible while her thoughts were in such turmoil.

'Are you all right?'

The soft, deep voice broke the silence, and Chrissie forced a shaky smile to her lips, knowing she couldn't afford to let him see how she felt.

'Yes . . . it just gave me a fright, that's all. Silly of me not to look where I was going.' She laughed, a thin, strained little laugh which sounded unnatural even to her own ears. 'I'm sorry to be so clumsy.'

'You could never be that,' he said quietly. 'Many things, maybe, but never clumsy.'

Chrissie felt herself go hot at the note in his deep voice. Her eyes dark with confusion, she stared silently at him and he smiled, the first real smile she'd ever seen him give; it was a revelation to her, as though she was suddenly seeing a quite different man from that hard, tough stranger. He looked so much younger, softer, less alarming and, heaven forbid she should admit it, wickedly attractive!

'Is that it, then, Jack? Have we finished for the morning, or are there any more to see?'

The voice calling from the wings broke the spell, and Chrissie hurriedly looked away, feeling thoroughly shaken. She'd come to the club with such clear-cut ideas of what she'd do and say, how she'd handle the situation, but little by little everything was starting to change. For all these weeks she'd been building up a picture of Jackson Knight, a picture based on her hatred of him and, up till a few minutes ago, she would have sworn she was right. But now . . . well, maybe now she'd just found out that the reality was somewhat different.

This was no standard, cardboard villain, a cut-out image with clearly defined edges and limits, but a real and very complex person. Down in black and white, neatly set out as an exercise on paper, she'd known exactly how to handle him, but faced with Jackson Knight in the flesh—well, that was a different thing entirely! She'd have to re-think . . . and fast!

Playing for time, she glanced across the stage to where a middle-aged man was waiting next to a huge bank of electrical switches. The very last thing she felt like doing at the moment was auditioning, but there was no way she could afford to chicken out. If it took every scrap of determination she possessed, she'd do it, and do it well, at that!

'Is that Mac?' she asked quickly, before her

nerve could fail her.

'Yes. As I said, he's in charge of all the lighting, and quite frankly, he's one of the best in the business. Just tell him what sort of effect you're aiming for, then you can safely leave it up to him.'

She nodded, her eyes not quite meeting the dark ones which were studying her so intently.

'Right then, I'll go and introduce myself and see what we can work out.'

She crossed the stage, forcing herself to move with an outward show of confidence while inside she was a quivering mass of jelly. The time had come, it was now or never, and she was going to make the most of it. She was going to give Jackson Knight a real run for his money!

The lights dimmed, the full, bright glare narrowing to a soft pool of brilliance, highlighting the small table set in the very centre of the stage. With a studied grace, Chrissie walked over and sat down behind it, taking her time to settle comfortably on the chair. This was the last of the tricks she intended to perform for the audition, and by far and away the most difficult. The timing for this had to be spot-on for it to work, yet suddenly she was filled brimful with confidence.

With the fluid, unhurried movements which were a magician's stock-in-trade, she reached under the edge of the table and drew out a handful of brilliantly coloured glass beads and scattered them across its silk-covered surface, waiting patiently till they settled into place. Looking up, she gave the briefest of nods, and immediately the stage was plunged into darkness, broken only by a single spot illuminating her pale, slender hands and the glowing pieces of glass.

She ran her hands slowly back and forth over the beads, gently moving them till they lay in a precisely neat line across the black silk. Her hands made one last sweep along the row, checking they were all in place, then she was ready. With a lightning-quick movement she raised her hands, relief surging through her as the line of beads followed to seemingly hover in the air. She paused for a second, then clapped her hands together, a tiny smile curving her lips as she heard the gasp from some unseen watcher as the line curved round to form a circle. The circle began to revolve, slowly at first, then faster and faster, till all that could be seen was a spinning kaleidoscope of rainbow colours and patterns flashing through the darkness. Magic—pure magic! Or so it would seem to the onlooker who couldn't see the complicated network of gossamer-fine wires which held it all together!

The drum roll she'd requested to accompany this part of her act was reaching a crescendo now, and for the second time Chrissie clapped her hands and the spinning circle stopped, then disintegrated as the beads fell to the table and scattered. Perfect!

The lights came on and she stood up to take a bow, smiling round at the half-dozen or so people who'd stopped to watch. From the corner of her eyes she caught sight of Jackson Knight coming towards her, and the smile froze on her lips. Everything had gone so well, but had it been good enough to get her the job? Heart pounding loud and hard in her chest, she waited to hear his verdict.

'When can you start?'

It was what she'd prayed for, what she'd hoped and planned and schemed for all these long weeks. Looking up, Chrissie smiled, a brilliant, beautiful smile, just for him . . . the man who had condemned her sister to prison!

CHAPTER THREE

THE BUS journey back to her flat took the best part of an hour, but Chrissie barely noticed the time passing, her every thought centred on what had happened that morning. Sitting stiffly erect, she stared sightlessly through the grimy window, letting the events replay through her mind and shivering with a sudden unquenchable fear.

Could she handle it, see the whole thing through? If anyone had asked her earlier, then her answer would have been a very definite 'yes', but now she wasn't quite that certain. Granted, the situation was still the same: Kate was still in prison awaiting trial on a charge of smuggling drugs into the country, and she was just as determined to prove her innocent, but it was her view of Jackson Knight which had altered, shifted slightly out of focus.

True, he'd been everything she'd expected and more, and it was the 'more' which really worried her. The ruthless side of him she'd allowed for, but the other side, that blatant, open attraction he'd shown her—well, that needed careful consideration, as did her quite unexpected response to it. She had to be honest and face up to the fact that, no matter how much she might loathe him for what he'd done, there was still something about the man which drew her. It might only be some sort of

strange chemistry, but it frightened her far more
than the daunting task which lay ahead; frightened
her, and confused the issue. Resting her head back
against the seat, she reviewed the facts, desperately
trying to get them back into perspective.

She'd been in Las Vegas when she'd first heard
about Kate, three weeks into one of the most
important engagements she'd been offered in her
career to date, and loving every moment of it. The
American audience had been more than just
receptive to her act, and the management of the
top nightclub had been tentatively suggesting
that they extend her contract for a further term.
The news, coming as it did via a telephone call
from her distraught mother, had shaken her to the
core.

Kate had been stopped coming through Customs
and, when searched, had been found to have over a
kilo of heroin concealed in her luggage. She'd been
arrested immediately and no bail had been set.
Chrissie had cancelled the rest of her booking and
flown home at once, knowing there was no way her
mother could cope with it all on her own. In her
sixties, her mother was frail and far from well;
there was no way she could have handled all the
stress of finding a solicitor for Kate, nor the strain
of travelling back and forth between her home in
the north-west and London, where Kate was being
held on remand.

Chrissie had gone straight from the airport to the
prison and, when she was eventually allowed to see
her sister, had been shocked by the changes just a
few days' imprisonment had wrought. Kate had

always been pale, her delicate colouring that of a typical redhead, but now she looked like death, with huge, smudgy shadows ringing lifeless green eyes. Her hair, always silkily soft and clean, had clung to her head, the greasy strands wildly dishevelled, as though they had not seen a brush for days. However, if the physical changes had shocked Chrissie, then it was her sister's attitude which had really worried her, making her realise that helping Kate could be an uphill struggle when she seemed so utterly determined not to help herself.

Time after time Chrissie had questioned her about the drugs, asked where she'd got them, if she'd known they were in her case, but Kate had steadfastly refused to answer. All she would say was that she was innocent and that it had all been a mistake. It had only been when Chrissie, in a final flare of exasperated temper, had accused her of shielding someone, that she'd finally reacted. Colour had flared under Kate's pale skin, tears had started to her eyes and she'd stood up, demanding to be returned to her cell. And that had been the first and only time that Chrissie had seen her.

When she'd returned to the prison the following day, she'd been politely but firmly told that her sister refused to see her and been turned away. Since then Kate had refused to see anyone except the solicitor hired to help sort out the whole wretched muddle. Kate was shielding someone, and there was no way she was going to say just who that person was, no matter what it cost her, and it could cost her dear! As the solicitor had been quick to point out, the sentence for smuggling drugs in such a quantity could be anything up to ten years.

Ten years! Chrissie had left the solicitor's office, her head reeling with the thought, and had known there and then that there was no way she would let her sister face ten years' imprisonment without a struggle. If Kate refused to be sensible and help herself, then she, Chrissie, would do it for her. She would find out who had used her, set her up as a courier, and see it was that person who took the blame.

She started her search by going to the flat Kate had shared with two other girls, then to the firm of stockbrokers where she'd worked as a secretary, but at both she met with the same reaction: a barely veiled hostility. No one wanted to help, to answer her questions about Kate's personal and business life, in case by doing so some of the scandal would rub off on them. Downhearted, she had returned home to the tiny village of Kings Moss, where her mother lived, and it had been there that she'd started to piece together the puzzle.

Some impulse had made her ask to read Kate's letters, and as she'd read them one name and one alone had jumped clean out of the page to assault her . . . Jackson Knight. Several times Kate had mentioned him, but it was the final letter her mother had received which contained the clues which Chrissie needed. The letter had been bubbling with excitement, the words running together in a crazy jumble, so that it had been a struggle to decipher them, a struggle not helped by the fact that Kate had taken to writing just the letter 'J' when she referred to Jackson Knight. However, finally, Chrissie had made sense of it all and realised that she'd just found the name of the person who had involved Kate in the whole sorry mess. Just reading the details had made her blood start to boil.

Knight had invited Kate to spend a few days with him in New York, and she'd accepted. He had arranged everything down to the smallest detail: Kate was to fly out and meet him there, spend four days at his apartment, then fly back home *alone*, as he had to stay on to finalise some business contracts. It had been the perfect set-up.

Reading that strangely tragic letter, with its false aura of happiness, Chrissie had known at once that the only person who could have involved Kate had been Knight. It was blatantly obvious from the letters that her sister was desperately in love with him, and that would explain why she'd refused to reveal his involvement and save herself. Love was blind, so the saying went, but re-reading all those glowing, happy words, Chrissie knew it must also be deaf and dumb as well!

Knight had used Kate from the beginning, yet the pity of it was that she would probably refuse to believe it. He'd done a good job of making Kate fall in love with him, but Chrissie had been determined not to let that love destroy her. She would find evidence against Jackson Knight and see that he was brought to trial, no matter how much her sister might hate her for doing it!

For several days Chrissie had tossed around the problem of how to get close enough to Knight to do it. It had to be some way which wouldn't arouse his suspicions. Then, one day, when she was sitting at the top of Shaley Brow, staring over the lush green countryside, brooding over it, the answer came to her. Kate had mentioned in her letters that Knight owned a nightclub, a top nightspot in fact, noted for both its gaming-tables and excellent cabaret. Remembering this had set Chrissie thinking. She had contacted her agent, explaining that she was looking for a new booking, and casually mentioned the name of Knights, explaining that she would be interested in anything that was going there as she'd heard about its excellent reputation. Her agent had taken the bait and, while not promising anything definite, had agreed to look into it.

Over a week passed and Chrissie had reached near-desperation point when finally he'd phoned to say that an audition had been arranged if she was still interested. Still interested? It had been all she could do to stop herself shouting for joy as she'd accepted the offer. She'd travelled down to London the following day and found herself a cheap room in one of the more rundown areas, knowing she couldn't afford to waste money on decent accommodation. Kate's bank balance had been frozen by the courts pending the trial, and as there was only what Chrissie and her mother had between them in savings to meet all the expenses, there was no way she could waste a single penny.

So she had taken the seedy bedsitter and spent two miserable days there, eaten up with worry, planning how to set about finding the evidence if she actually got the job. She'd covered sheet after sheet of paper with detailed plans on how to go about it, but now staring through the bus window, Chrissie realised she might as well throw them all on the fire. There was no way she could plot and plan, work out all the finer details, when Jackson Knight had turned out to be . . . well, so totally unpredictable. She would have to wait, play the whole thing by ear and hope her pitch was perfect!

The bus slewed round a corner, slamming her shoulder painfully against the metal window-frame, and with a start she realised she'd almost daydreamed herself past her stop. She pushed her way down the crowded aisle and freed her case from the baggage rack, then clung grimly to the handrail as the bus lurched to a halt. She jumped off, then waited till it pulled away from the stop before crossing the busy main road.

The room she'd rented was one of some half-dozen crammed into the floors above a takeaway food store and, opening the outer door, she felt her stomach lurch at the sickening smell of rancid fat. She hurried up the stairs to her room and closed the door thankfully behind her. It had been a long, disturbing morning and, though this room with its shabby furniture was a long way from her idea of heaven, it seemed to offer sanctuary, a place where she could get her thoughts together and review the situation.

She shivered, cold rippling and eddying through her body. Had she done right by taking the job, or had she just given herself a whole load of trouble? She had no idea, not that it really made any difference. No, the die had been cast the minute she'd found out whom Kate was protecting, and there was no way she could change the way it was now set to roll. Come what may, she would find what she needed, but deep down she felt it could be a bitterly hard task. Jackson Knight was nobody's fool; she would have to be very careful how she went about things if she wasn't to arouse his suspicions. After all, she was moving into his territory, the enemy camp, and as far as she could see he held all the weapons . . . or did he?

She crossed the room and stared into the small, square mirror hung over the mantel, studying the soft curve of her cheeks, the full ripeness of her lips, the silken waves of honey-blonde hair, and smiled a trifle grimly.

There was one weapon she had, just one . . . herself! Knight wanted her and she would use that fact, the one weapon left in her arsenal, to destroy him. So, let battle commence!

Three days later, however, struggling to pull the heavy cases full of costumes from the back of the taxi, Chrissie was far less confident of her ability to engage in warfare. True, she'd armoured herself as best she could by dressing in a deep coral skirt and jacket which did wonderful things for her golden colouring and slender figure, but was it really enough? Surely she needed something more than mere appearance to fight with? It seemed so little to take on a man like Knight, such a fragile sort of weapon. How on earth could she ever hope to win?

'Here, let me take those for you.'

The rich, deep voice made her jump. With a start, she spun round to find Jackson Knight standing beside her, and her jaw dropped just a fraction as she took in his appearance. Dressed in a deep charcoal suit with fine white silk shirt, he looked so different from what she remembered that for a few seconds Chrissie could only stare at him in dumbfounded wonder.

'Well?' he queried, a mocking tilt to his dark brows, and she flushed, realising she was standing in the middle of the pavement ogling him like some poor smitten admirer. Turning away, she pulled a note from her wallet to pay the driver, too confused by Knight's unexpected appearance to query the exorbitant amount he charged her.

'Ready?'

Without waiting for an answer, Knight picked up the cases and strode into the club. Slowly, reluctantly, Chrissie followed. Her head was spinning, a jumbled, confused flurry of images whirling inside her, and she desperately tried to get her thoughts back into some sort of sensible order. After all, what hope did she have of achieving her objective if she allowed a mere change in appearance to throw her? No, she had to remember the one basic fact that, despite all this new suave sophistication, he was the same person, the same man who'd used her sister.

The thought steadied her, gave her the strength to walk calmly through the door he held propped open with his shoulder, and into the hallway. Glancing round, she let her eyes linger on all the expensive fittings, deliberately whipping up the

same deep feeling of revulsion she'd felt on her
first visit. There was no way she could afford to
soften, to allow anything to come between her and
what she knew had to be done. There were just
four weeks left until Kate came to trial, just four
short weeks to find the evidence she needed to clear
her, and there was no way she could waste a
minute. Turning, she smiled warmly at him.

'Thank you for helping me, Mr Knight. It was
kind of you.'

'My pleasure entirely.'

Just for a second, a fleeting hint of warmth lit
his dark eyes, a mere tiny spark, but to Chrissie it
was as revealing as any neon signboard. Quickly
she glanced away, frightened he'd see the triumph
which surged through her as she read its meaning.
For the past few days she'd spent hour after endless
hour going over everything he'd said to her, every
look and every gesture, praying she'd not been
mistaken in her belief that he was attracted to her.
Now, having seen that betraying glimmer, she
knew she'd been right. Jackson Knight was
attracted to her, it was a plain and indisputable
fact, and one that she would use to her advantage.
She would nurse that spark, fan it into a huge,
raging fire, then stand back and watch it destroy
him!

Filled with a strange feeling of power, she
crossed the few yards which separated them and
took one of the cases from his grasp, her fingers
brushing gently against his in a wholly
premeditated action.

'Sorry.'

Looking up from under the length of her dark lashes, she smiled at him, her expression as softly alluring as she could make it.

'Don't mention it,' he responded gently. His voice was low, perfectly even, but just for a moment Chrissie wondered if there was a touch of ironic amusement to it and chided herself for being careless. While most men would happily be taken in by sweet, girlish gestures, Jackson Knight definitely wasn't one of them. Instinct told her he was far too experienced for those sort of blatant tactics. No, it would need a far subtler approach than a lot of eyelash-batting to gain the result she was after, and she would have to remember it.

Taking the case briskly from him, she said firmly, 'I'm sure I must be keeping you from something, so if you'll just tell me where I can put my things, then I won't detain you further.'

'I've just come back from a meeting, actually, so the next hour or so is free. However, if you'll come with me I'll show you which dressing-room you can use while you're working here.'

He led the way through the hall and along one of the back corridors, shortening his stride to match Chrissie's, which was hampered by the pencil slimness of her coral skirt. Swapping the heavy case from one cramped hand to the other, she strove to keep pace with him, determined to start immediately in her search for evidence. There was a lot she needed to know about Jackson Knight, and now was as good a time as any to start.

'It sounds as if you're busy, then; does running the club take up all your time?'

He shot her a brief glance, his eyes dark as they studied her face, and she carefully pinned an expression of mere polite interest into place. It wouldn't do to let him know just how curious she really was about his business dealings, especially the non-legitimate ones!

'This club is only part of my business interests. Knights is now a worldwide operation, with holdings as far apart as Hong Kong and Sweden.'

'Is it?' It was impossible to keep the surprise from her voice, and Chrissie didn't bother trying. 'I hadn't realised . . . I mean, I just assumed there was this club and that was it.'

'No, not now. The club was the first, of course. My father started it about thirty years ago, but recently we've expanded into hotel and leisure complexes, though the majority of them offer gaming and cabaret facilities along with everything else. Knights aims to offer a client everything he requires on holiday, whether it be a morning workout in the gymnasium or a nightly flutter at the blackjack tables.'

'And it's successful?' she queried softly.

'Extremely. The meeting I was at this morning was for our shareholders, and I can honestly say that they were delighted with the company's progress. Knights is a very prosperous concern,' he added, almost drily.

'And you handle it all yourself? You own the whole thing, or at least the major part of the shares?'

'No. I have overall control of the business, but the stock is owned jointly by my brother and myself.'

'But you make all the decisions,' she insisted, determined to get a full picture of the operation.

'Oh, yes. Nothing goes on at Knights without me issuing the orders.'

There was a hint of ruthlessness to his tone, and Chrissie glanced away, suddenly sickened by the implications of the statement. To expand the company from one club to the huge concern he'd just told her about had taken not only business ability but a great deal of money. Where had all the money come from? That was the question, and one which she had the feeling she knew the answer to. Drugs had supplied the money for Knights' rapid expansion, and it had been Jackson Knight who had taken the decision to use them.

'I see,' she murmured.

'Do you?'

Stopping outside one of the dressing-rooms, he put the case down and turned towards her, a strange expression on his face. 'You seem very interested in everything, but why, I wonder?'

Chrissie halted, her heart bumping painfully against her ribs as she tried to think up a suitable answer.

'I . . . I'm always interested in the places where I work,' she finally managed, hating the lameness of the excuse.

'Are you?'

Taking the other case from her unresisting fingers, he set it down, then gently caught her hands in his and held them. 'And that's the only reason, is it?' he queried, his voice deep and gentle.

Forcing herself to meet his gaze, Chrissie stared back at him, feeling the warm strength of his fingers curled round hers. Deep down she knew she should feel repulsed by his touch, should be revolted that this man who'd built an empire on the suffering of others was holding her this way, but she wasn't. Revulsion just wasn't the name for this strange feeling of awareness which curled in tingling spirals through her body.

'Well?' he prompted.

With a mighty effort Chrissie forced her brain back into action, knowing she couldn't allow the undeniable physical attraction which ran between them to affect her in this crazy, dangerous way. Freeing her hands, she stepped back a pace, forcing a lightness to her voice when she spoke that she was far from feeling.

'But of course. What else could it be?'

With a tiny laugh she turned the door-handle and went to walk inside, halting abruptly as he caught her arm.

'So it's just that, is it? Not the fact that you're as attracted to me as I am to you?'

The boldness of the question stunned her, stealing her breath, so that for a moment she was unable to think of an answer. Then slowly a white-hot fury started to boil inside her. Of all the arrogant, conceited, big-headed . . . She opened her mouth, ready to tell him in no uncertain terms what she thought of this crazy notion, when a tiny voice of reason whispered in her ear. It was the opening she needed, the first shot in the battle, and she would be a fool to waste such valuable ammunition.

She stared back at him, her eyes brilliantly blue as they met his dark ones and whispered softly, 'Maybe.'

She stepped round the cases and walked into the room, feeling the tiny, gentle word hit home with all the impact of a bullet!

The rehearsals passed with excruciating slowness. The whole time Chrissie was going through her routine, she was aware of Jackson Knight watching her. He'd removed the suit jacket and rolled back the cuffs of his shirt, making it easier to relate him to the man she'd met previously, yet, somehow, she still felt far too aware of him to be comfortable. It wasn't as though he spoke or did anything to claim her attention, but he was just there, a dark, brooding presence it was impossible to ignore. Glancing sideways for the umpteenth time, she caught his gaze and forced a smile to her lips, knowing she couldn't let him see how much he disturbed her. No, if she was really attracted to him, as she'd so recently and rashly implied, then she would feel flattered by such a display of undivided attention, not terrified!

'Right then, Miss Lane. I think that's it.'

Mac's voice, with its soft Scottish burr, was the sweetest sound she'd heard for ages, offering welcome relief from the situation. She smiled at him, her face lit with genuine appreciation for all the care he'd taken working out the lighting she would need.

'Thanks, Mac, I'm really grateful for all your

trouble; and by the way, the name's Chrissie.'

He nodded, turning back to his switches, but not before she'd glimpsed the flush of pleasure which tinged his lined cheeks. Not wishing to embarrass him further, she gathered her belongings together and packed them swiftly and carefully into a metal-bound trunk and the drawstring bag. Props were expensive, and it had taken her several years to build up this collection. There was no way she could risk having them damaged, even though every instinct was screaming at her to bundle them up and run. From the corner of her eyes she could see Knight approaching, and the tension which had been simmering gently for the past hour boiled over. What would he say? What sort of follow-up would there be to her earlier, blatant encouragement?

'Right, then. I've been timing your act, and I'm afraid it's going to be at least five minutes short. You'll need to add something for both shows. Will that cause a problem?'

He glanced down at the sheaf of notes he was holding, mercifully missing her stunned gasp of amazement and sheer, undiluted mortification. While she'd been imagining him standing there, filled with lustful thoughts and admiration, the reality was that he'd been more concerned about getting full value for his money! A wave of slightly hysterical laughter bubbled up inside her, and she swallowed hard to force it down. Maybe she wasn't as good at playing the vamp as she'd so confidently imagined, if work had been the main thing on his mind!

'Well?'

'I . . . I . . .' Pulling herself sternly together, she said shortly, 'There's no problem. I can add a card trick in to each performance to cover the extra minutes.'

She knew her voice sounded stiff and formal, but frankly there was little she could do about it. He'd taken so much wind out of her sails with that blunt statement that it was lucky she'd found enough left to answer. Annoyance rippled through her as she remembered all the uncomfortable minutes she'd just spent, and she stared coldly back at him.

'Right, that sounds fine. Thank you.'

She nodded, still too incensed by her own stupidity to speak. She caught hold of the case and bag and started for the dressing-room, pausing reluctantly as he spoke.

'Just one thing before you go . . . Chrissie.'

His voice was low, rich as treacle, with just the tiniest emphasis on her name that made her spine stiffen and her toes tingle.

'Yes?' she snapped, sparing him the briefest of glances over her shoulder.

'Just that I never mix business with pleasure, no matter how tempting the idea seems. There's a time and a place for everything.'

There was no mistaking his meaning, no mistaking the barely veiled sensuality which laced his voice, and she flushed. Turning away, she strode rapidly across the stage, ruing the day she'd ever seen his name. Still, when this was all over and Jackson Knight was safely behind bars where he belonged, then she would wipe him from her mind . . . forever!

It was a comforting thought, or should have been if that tiny, nagging little voice which seemed to be making its presence felt of late hadn't whispered once more softly in her ear. Flouncing into the dressing-room, she slammed the door hard to obliterate the sound, but it refused to be silenced and rose to a full-throated roar.

Would she really be able to shut Knight out of her life so easily now that she'd let him in?

The answer to the question terrified her, and she stared round the room in sudden desperation. She had to get out of here, get a few hours away from the club and all its problems, but where should she go? Glancing at her watch, she realised with a jolt that it was already two-thirty: far too late to bother making the long journey back to the bedsit, when she had to be back here by seven. What could she do to fill the intervening hours?

For a few minutes she stood undecided in the middle of the small room, till the low rumblings of her empty stomach made the decision for her. She'd been so keyed up that morning that she'd skipped breakfast, but there was no way she could go much longer without a meal. What she'd do was find a snack-bar, have a late lunch, then browse through the shops till it was time to return for the first performance. It would mean a long and tiring day, but frankly anything was better than sitting here worrying.

Glad that she'd arrived at a decision, she slipped on her jacket and flicked a comb through the ends of her hair. Her lipstick had faded, so she quickly outlined her lips in the soft coral tint which was only a shade or two paler than her outfit. The suit had been wickedly expensive but, skimming a glance over her reflection, Chrissie knew that it had been worth every penny. It was just a pity that it would only be the patrons of the nearest, cheapest snack-bar who reaped the benefit!

Picking up the soft cream leather bag which matched her high-heeled sandals, she left the room and walked swiftly along the corridor. Everywhere was very quiet, as though the building was completely deserted, and unconsciously she found herself stepping lightly to preserve the silence. Most of the staff would have gone home by now, to return later for the evening opening. Had Jackson Knight followed their example, or was he still here, somewhere in this building?

The thought hovered at the edges of her mind, teasing and tormenting so that her footsteps slowed. She glanced round, suddenly realising that she'd reached the back hall and that the door to Knight's office was a mere half-dozen paces away. Was he in there, working at that big, mahogany desk, or had he left? It was suddenly imperative that she knew the answer, because if he had left then here was the chance she needed to search his office. He must have papers, records of his transactions, and what better place to keep them than the office? If she could just uncover some evidence, no matter how small, about his involvement in the drugs, then surely the police would have to take things further? She had to try, no matter how much the thought frightened her.

She rubbed her damp hands together, then rapped firmly on the door, waiting with heart pounding for an answer, but none came. There seemed to be no one there, so should she risk it and go in? For a second she hesitated, then slowly reached out and turned the handle, fighting down the sudden vivid memory of what had happened the last time she'd done that. If the room was in darkness, as it had been then, then, frankly, no power on earth would induce her to enter!

There was a light on; just a dim glow from a desk-lamp which barely broke the gloom in the windowless room, but enough to quell the worst of Chrissie's terrors. Glancing round, she checked nobody was watching her from the corridor, then hurried inside, closing the door firmly behind her.

'"Come into my parlour," said the spider to the fly . . .' well, right at that moment she knew just how that poor old fly had been feeling! Knight might be absent, but his presence lay like a tangible web over the whole room, making the back of her neck prickle in fearful anticipation. What if he came back? What reason could she give for being there this time?

For a full thirty seconds fear held her captive in its sticky web till slowly common sense returned. The longer she stood there dithering, then the greater the chance would be that she'd get caught. She had to get on with it, search the room, then get out as fast as she could. If she worked swiftly and quietly, then she'd be quite safe.

Somewhat reassured, she tried the filing cabinet

drawers but they were locked. Where would he keep the key? In his pocket, or somewhere in the room for convenience? It was a fifty-fifty chance; poor odds really, but the best on offer, so she would have to take them. She hurried forwards and pulled the top drawer of the desk open, searching rapidly through the neat piles of papers, but found no sign of any keys. She pulled out the next drawer to repeat the process, cursing softly under her breath as it jammed against the runners. Hands shaking, she wrenched it free, wincing as the wood shrieked in protest at such rough treatment.

'Who's there?'

The sudden question startled her so much that she jumped, her stomach lurching sickeningly with shock. Glancing wildly round, she searched the room to see where it had come from, and every single cell in her body froze as she noticed the door which was standing partly open. Painted in the same uniformly drab cream shade as the walls, she'd never noticed it on her earlier visit, never realised till now that a second room led off from this one. Now, with the door open, she could see the back of a green leather couch and, cushioned against it, a head of midnight-dark hair.

Although she could see little besides this glimpse, Chrissie needed nothing more to identify Jackson Knight and her blood ran cold. Slowly, carefully, she slid the drawer back into place and inched her way round the desk. She had to get out of here—and fast! Heart pounding, she ran across the room, her footsteps muffled by the thick carpet.

'Is that you, Thompson?'

There was the sound of leather creaking, a
muffled grunt, and in that instant Chrissie knew
she wouldn't make it. There was no way she could
get out of the room and along the corridor without
him seeing her, no way at all. She would have to
stay and face him!

CHAPTER FOUR

'DID YOU manage to get those . . . Chrissie!'

Astonishment crossed Knight's face as he spotted her standing by the door, and instinctively Chrissie knew she had to act quickly before it faded. Leaning back, she pushed firmly against the door as though to close it.

'I'm dreadfully sorry, Mr Knight, but I thought you must have heard me knock. Am I disturbing you?' She moved further into the room and smiled at him, her expression as softly guileless as she could make it.

'No . . . I . . . I . . .' He flicked a glance at the desk, and she held her breath, wondering what he'd come up with. He must have heard that drawer being wrenched open, but would he think he'd just imagined it? Her hands were curled into fists, and she forced herself to relax, knowing that any sign of tension would only promote his suspicions. She had to act naturally, stick to the pretence that she'd only just entered the room, or she'd be finished.

He swung back to face her, his eyes intent, then, raising his hands, he rubbed them over his face, kneading at his eyes as though they were troubling him.

'Are you all right?' she asked.

He smiled briefly at her, and with a start of

surprise she realised just how drawn and pale he looked.

'Yes. It's just this damned headache which refuses to budge. My own fault, of course: too many late nights working on figures. I was just sitting down resting my eyes when I heard a noise in here.'

For a second a flicker of suspicion crossed his face, and Chrissie spoke quickly before it had time to deepen.

'You must have heard me knocking, and that's what disturbed you. Have you taken anything for your headache yet?'

'No. I sent Thompson out to get me some aspirins, but heaven knows where he's got to.' He shot a glance at his watch, then stared once again at the desk, his face puzzled.

'My mother gets dreadful headaches. She usually finds that the only way to shift them is to have her head and neck massaged.'

'Is that an offer?'

Was it? For a second Chrissie could have bitten her wayward tongue off for uttering such a rash statement. It had just been a way of filling in silence, a means of diverting his thoughts from the desk and the sounds he'd heard, and as such had been alarmingly successful! His attention was now fixed firmly in her direction, and nothing could hide the sudden gleam which lit his dark eyes. With a sinking feeling she realised she'd just talked herself into a corner. If she backed down now, then instinct told her it wouldn't take more than five seconds for that gleam to change to the cold glint of suspicion. Slipping the bag from her shoulder, she hung it over the back of a chair, forcing herself to act as naturally as possible.

'If you think it might help, I'd be glad to give it a try, but you'll have to sit down and relax for it to be even half-way successful.'

'Right, let's go back in here.'

He led her through into the adjoining room, sweeping a hand round to indicate the couch and matching chair. 'Where do you want me to sit to make it easiest for you?'

Glancing quickly round the small room, she nodded towards the chair. 'That looks fine.'

He sat down, settling himself comfortably back in the chair, his dark eyes following her movements as she stripped off her jacket. Pushing up the sleeves of her silky-knit sweater, she walked round behind him, glad to escape his disturbing gaze. Heaven knew how she'd survive the next few minutes when even the thought of touching him was making her tremble. She must be mad to have agreed . . . mad or desperate!

'Shall I loosen the neck of my shirt for you?'

'Please.' Her voice was a mere croak, and she swallowed hard to ease the knot of tension. Rubbing her hands together, she watched while he flicked the top buttons of his silk shirt open, pulling the collar away from the tanned column of his throat.

'Will that do?'

'Mmm.' It was suddenly impossible to answer with words when her mouth had gone as dry as a desert. Glancing down, she strove to keep her gaze centred on the back of his dark head and away from the tantalising glimpses of hair-sprinkled chest showing through the partly opened shirt, but it was a strangely difficult task.

'Ready when you are.' Leaning back, he closed his eyes, and slowly Chrissie started the massage, her fingers clumsy with nerves till gradually they found a rhythm. Many years ago she'd learned the art of head and neck massage, knowing it was virtually the only way to relieve the migraine headaches from which her mother suffered, and now she found her old skill returning.

Slowly she stroked his temples, her slender fingers gently soothing the throbbing pulse. Then she worked her hands over his head, rubbing in a smooth circular motion which was intensely soothing, and heard him sigh in pleasure. Delicately she eased her hands down the back of his neck, the balls of her thumbs rubbing gently but firmly at the tense muscles at the base of his head, feeling the way they gradually relaxed under her touch. Moving downwards, she slid her hands under his collar, her palms flattening against the warm muscles of his shoulders while her fingers delicately kneaded the smooth flesh. As though they had a life of their own, her hands worked deftly on and on, and Chrissie was barely aware of time passing till he spoke.

'This is heaven, but you must be tired.'

Was she? For a moment she stood quite still, her hands resting limply against his body while she considered the statement. She'd been so engrossed in the massage, so caught up with the rhythm, the feel of her fingers sliding over his warm, smooth skin, that she'd never even noticed her arms were aching. Touching him had felt good, so good that she'd never wanted it to end!

The realisation shocked her so much that she jumped back, snatching her hands away from his shoulders and rubbing them together as though to wipe away the feel of his skin.

'I am a bit tired now . . . but I hope it's helped.'

Her voice sounded strangely high-pitched and breathless, but she refused to wonder about the reason for it. She walked round the chair and picked up her jacket, her pulse racing as he came and took it from her. Slowly he guided it up her arms then smoothed it over her shoulders, his hands lingering just a fraction more than was really necessary.

'You're trembling, Chrissie. Why?' His voice was low and so gentle that it made her start to ache deep inside. For a moment she swayed back against him, suddenly yearning to feel his hands touching her skin the same way hers had just touched him.

'Why, Chrissie?'

His warm breath clouded her ear, and she was filled with a wave of confusion. What was happening to her? Why did she feel like this, as though every part of her had turned to water? Half turning to him, she licked her dry lips, feeling and seeing the flicker which raced through his body as his eyes followed the movement of her tongue.

'Jackson, I . . . I . . .'

'Hey, Mr Knight, I've got those pills. They're on your desk.'

The sudden shout, followed by the sound of the office door slamming, broke the spell and, with a startled gasp, Chrissie pulled away. She ran through to the office and, snatching up her bag, clutched it to her like a shield. Her heart was hammering, her pulse was popping, her knees were trembling; she must be mad!

'Just a minute.'

Knight had followed her and was standing just inside the doorway, a frown creasing his wide brow.

'Yes.' It was impossible to meet his gaze, and she looked down, studying her nervous fingers which were twisting the soft leather strap into ribbons.

'Thank you, for the massage. You have magic hands, you know; my headache's almost gone, so I won't be needing those aspirins after all.' He shot a wry glance at the small bottle standing on the edge of the desk. 'It's a shame that Thompson brought them, really.'

There was a double edge to the statement, and Chrissie flicked a nervous glance towards the door. There was no way she wanted to discuss what had happened, no way she wanted to admit to herself what she'd been feeling, at least not now. Maybe later, in the peace and quiet of her own room, then she'd be able to deal with it, work out some acceptable explanation for that sudden surge of longing which had filled her, but definitely not now! Slowly she edged towards the door.

'That's quite all right, Mr Knight. I'm just glad it's helped.'

'Oh, it has, but, Chrissie, do me a favour, will

you?'

'What?'

'Forget the "Mr Knight", will you, sweetheart? The name is Jackson, Jack to my real friends. After all, you did manage it before.'

There was a teasing note to his deep voice, and she flushed, the colour stealing up her cheeks in a delicate pink tide. He laughed, the rich sound filling the room so that she shot a swift glance at him, startled.

'Oh, Chrissie, you're priceless, do you know that?'

'What do you mean?' she demanded, stiffening.

'It's just that you're such an odd mixture of allure and innocence. I don't think I've met anyone like you before in the whole of my life. It's difficult to tell which is the real woman.'

'I'm sorry——' she began, but he interrupted swiftly.

'Don't be.' Crossing the room, he ran a finger lightly down the curve of her cheek. 'It's a beguiling mixture, you know. It intrigues me, so don't be sorry . . . ever.' Bending, he pressed his lips to hers in the lightest, softest of kisses, then drew back, his eyes dark and unfathomable as they stared into hers. 'Don't ever be sorry for what you are. I hope you never change.'

For a few seconds they stared at each other in silence before he turned away. Raising her hand, Chrissie ran a trembling finger over her lips, feeling shaken. She'd been kissed before, many times and far more passionately, so why had that kiss made such a deep impression?

'By the way, what did you want to see me for?'

'Pardon?' For a long blank minute she stared at him, her mind still full of the heady memory of that kiss.

'Well, I assume you did have a reason for coming to the office before. What was it?'

Maybe if he'd asked her that a few minutes earlier, before all her senses had been set topsy-turvy, then she'd have been able to come up with some sort of reasonable answer, but just at the moment . . . well! Why had she come, or at least, what reason could she give him? Desperately her mind raced over a few dozen possible excuses, then found a flaw in every single one of them. She had to say something, but what?

'Well, I . . .' she stumbled, the next part of the story escaping her.

'Yes?' He was watching her, a lingering amusement softening his face, but for how long? How long would it be before that softness turned to the harshness of suspicion, followed by anger? By her reckonings, no more than a few minutes. She had to think up something quick.

'I was just going out for some lunch and . . .' Oh, lord, how should she continue?

'And?' he prompted.

'And I thought I'd just call in to see if . . .'

'To see if I wanted to join you,' he finished for her.

Well, it hadn't been exactly number one on her list of possible excuses, nor even number two or three, but if he was happy with it, then who was she to argue? Fixing him with her most beguiling smile, she said nothing.

'Don't be shy about asking, Chrissie, I'm flattered. I'll just get my jacket.'

Get his jacket! Now, that was carrying things a little too far. She searched desperately for an excuse to cancel this unexpected and unwelcome lunch-date, and came up with something which seemed perfectly valid.

'Actually, I think it's a bit too late now, don't you? It's already way past three, so most places will be closed. Perhaps we should leave it till another day.' She forced just the right amount of regret to her tone, not too little and not too much.

'Nonsense, of course it's not too late. I know the perfect place.' He picked up his jacket and shrugged it on.

'You do?' Horror added a sharpness to her voice, and she bit her lip as she saw him throw her a startled glance. 'Where?' she asked, a touch more softly.

'My flat, of course. I make a mean omelette, and the best thing is that it will be peaceful there, with no other people to disturb us.'

He smiled as he held the door open for her, and slowly Chrissie walked through it, understanding for the first time in her life just how a condemned prisoner must feel on his way to the gallows!

He led her briskly along the corridors to the back courtyard, pausing to lock the heavy outer door behind them, and Chrissie shivered as the warmth of the sun drifted over her cold skin. Tiny ripples of shock were curling through her, making it difficult to think, but she had to try, had to work

out how to handle the next few hours. Granted, on
the face of it everything seemed clear-cut, a simple
lunch-date, but what else was on the menu besides
the promised omelette? Was she to be dessert?

The idea terrified her, all the more so because
there was little she could do about it. If he did
make a pass at her and she slapped him down, then
everything she'd planned on would be ruined. Yet
if she didn't, if she actually encouraged him, then
there was just no knowing where it could all lead
to. Jackson Knight was no inexperienced boy, he
was a man with a man's desires. Would she be able
to handle him? In fact, if it came down to it, could
she really make the ultimate sacrifice and give
herself to him to save Kate?

'You're very quiet. Are you feeling all right?'

The soft-voiced question broke through her
tormented thoughts, and Chrissie stiffened,
flicking a nervous glance in his direction.

'Are you ill?' Reaching out, he laid the back of
his hand gently against her cheek and instinctively
she shied away, her nerves too raw to cope with
even this brief contact.

'No, I'm fine,' she answered quickly. 'I was just
a bit dazzled by the sun, that's all.'

'Sure?'

'Yes, of course.'

'Good. I was going to suggest we leave it if you
aren't feeling too good, but it seems we won't have
to. Come along.'

He slid his hand under her elbow to guide her
across the yard, and Chrissie had to fight to control
a sudden urge to scream with annoyance. He'd all

but handed her an excuse to get out of this lunch-date, and what had she done? Turned it down flat! How could she ever have been so dumb? Seething with frustration, she walked stiffly beside him, feeling the warm strength of his fingers fastened round her arm like a shackle.

'Here we are.' He pulled a bunch of keys from his pocket and unlocked a door set into the far wall of the club, a tiny smile curving his long lips as he saw the puzzlement which crossed her face.

'Where are you taking me?' she demanded, stopping dead and viewing the open door with as much enthusiasm as she would a gaping coffin.

'Up to my flat, of course.'

'Your flat,' she echoed blankly.

'Yes. Didn't you know that I live above the club?'

'No. I had no idea.'

With a hollow feeling in the pit of her stomach, she followed him inside and up the narrow staircase which led into the flat. That he might live above the club had never occurred to her before. Now, however, it presented a hitherto unconsidered problem: if he was on the premises, both day and night, then how would she ever get the chance to search the place thoroughly? It was something she would have to think about and make plans for, but not now. Now she had to concentrate on getting through this lunch-date . . . unscathed.

She followed him into the lounge, pausing just inside the doorway to look round, suddenly curious to see where he lived. Experts claimed that you could learn a lot about a person by studying their home surroundings; was it true? She hoped so. She could do with all the help she could get to find out what made Jackson Knight tick.

It wasn't an exceptionally large room, but the two floor-to-ceiling windows let in so much light that it felt incredibly spacious, a feeling heightened by the clever choice of colours and furnishings. The walls were tinted a soft, pale green, a delicate shade like water flowing over mossy stones. Scatter rugs of green, beige and softest pink made islands of colour against the buffed sheen of the wooden plank floor. Two creamy tweed couches faced one another across the width of a low wooden table, their bareness alleviated by mounds of pastel cushions heaped in the corners. A huge bowl of roses on the centre of the table lent a heady fragrance to the air, tantalising her nostrils. It was a beautiful room, uncluttered yet strangely welcoming, and so unlike the décor to be found downstairs that Chrissie was stunned into silence. It was hard to imagine that the same person could have chosen all that rich baroqueness and this exquisite simplicity.

'Like it?' Slipping off his jacket, Jackson tossed it over the back of the couch then turned towards her, his dark eyes studying her expression. She swallowed hard, forcing a smile to her lips, knowing she was now more puzzled than ever. Far from giving her a clue to what he was really like, the room had just confused her even more.

'Yes. It's lovely.'

'But?' he queried softly.

'But nothing . . . it's just . . . well, I suppose it's just so different from the club that I'm surprised. Silly really, I know. You probably chose the furnishings downstairs for a purpose: to give a feeling of richness to the place. There's no reason why I should have assumed your home would be similar.'

'Yes, it is different, very different, thank heavens, but not because I chose to make it like that. My brother was responsible for the club's décor. He chose everything.'

His voice was flat, even, yet there was something in its tone which startled her. She glanced quickly at his face, studying the tight, uncompromising line of his lips, the sudden harshness, and knew in that instant there was something terribly wrong between him and his brother. Call it sixth sense, call it instinct, call it anything you liked, but she just knew. Yet what was it? What had happened between them to bring that look of hatred to his face? She was suddenly filled with an insatiable desire to find out.

'Where is your brother?' she asked quietly. 'I remember you telling me that you both have equal shares in the company, so does he work here with you?'

She kept her voice just politely curious, biting back the urgency which raced through her. It might be fanciful, but deep down she had the strangest feeling that his answer could be important to her. Had they quarrelled over some family matter, mere sibling rivalry, or had it been over something entirely different, the business or maybe even

Jackson's involvement in drugs?

'No, Jonathan doesn't work here any longer. He's based over in the States, in charge of a new complex we've recently opened.'

'Is he younger or older than you?' she asked, desperate to keep him talking. With a studied nonchalance she crossed the room to examine a delicate watercolour, barely seeing the clever brushwork and expert use of colour. Every tiny bit of her attention was centred on Jackson Knight, ready to absorb each nuance and inflection in his deep voice. Was this the first clue she needed, the first of many keys to Kate's freedom? She could only hope.

'Younger, two years younger. We're not blood brothers, though: I was adopted.'

'Adopted!'

Chrissie swung round, giving up any pretence of interest in the painting, and stared at him, her blue eyes mirroring her surprise. He smiled, a sad, slow smile which for some reason tugged at her heartstrings, making her ache.

'Yes. My parents believed that they couldn't have children, so adopted me, then a couple of years later along came Jonathan. It was what they'd always dreamed of, a child of their own.'

'But surely it didn't make any difference to you, did it? You were still their child.'

He shrugged, his heavy shoulders moving briefly under the thin pale silk. 'Maybe, maybe not. Who can tell? Anyway, enough about me and my family. I'm starving, so how about giving me a hand getting that lunch ready?'

He held his hand out to her, smiling, and instinctively Chrissie stepped forwards and slid her slim fingers into his. He'd changed the subject neatly and deftly, but nothing could erase the lingering echo of hurt which had been in his voice. Suddenly she was overwhelmed with compassion for the boy who'd felt himself unloved, the boy who'd become this man.

'I'm sure they still loved you just as much after your brother was born,' she said softly.

'Are you? I hope so, but it's something I'll never know for sure. But, Chrissie, thank you.'

'For what?'

'For caring enough to want me to believe it.'

For a second they stared at each other in silence, and Chrissie could see a tiny image of herself mirrored in his eyes, knew that his image must likewise be mirrored in hers. It was only there for a moment, a tiny heartbeat of time, but it seemed to link them together, as though an invisible bond had been forged between them . . . forever.

The omelette was light, fluffy and packed with tempting slivers of cheese and ham, yet to Chrissie it tasted little better than sawdust. She took a sip of the pale wine in her glass, feeling it trickle coldly down her hot, tight throat, then pushed a small piece of egg round her plate in a pretence of eating. Her earlier hunger had gone, driven away by that brief moment of understanding they'd shared earlier, a moment she desperately wished had never happened.

She didn't want to feel any sort of affinity with

this man, didn't want to acknowledge any sort of bond. Physical attraction was one thing and, though disturbing, could be reasoned out and handled, but an emotional tie was something she couldn't afford. Knight was the enemy, the person she must destroy to save Kate; there could be no room in her dealings with him for compassion. If she allowed herself to become involved on an emotional level, then she would be courting disaster.

'Not hungry?' He leant back in his chair, his eyes faintly curious as they studied her barely touched plate, and Chrissie hastily forced a thin smile to her lips.

'No, I'm sorry, but I seem to have lost my appetite for some reason, though the omelette was delicious.'

'Never mind. How about dessert or some coffee?'

'No, thank you. I'm fine, really; I don't want anything else.'

The desire to get away was suddenly so overwhelmingly strong that Chrissie had to hold herself rigid to stop herself from fleeing from the flat. With a lurching jolt all her former fears about what might happen after the meal came rushing back, and she gripped the edges of her chair in near panic.

'Nonsense, of course you must have a cup of coffee. Don't worry about keeping me from work, I usually take what's left of the afternoon off till it's time to open for the evening. After all, what's that saying about all work and no play making

Jack a dull boy? Well, I don't want that to happen, now, do I?'

He was teasing her, but Chrissie felt little able to appreciate it at the moment. There was nothing dull about this 'Jack', far from it, and that was a large part of the problem! Heaven alone knew what sort of games he would want to play!

'No, I really must be going. It's been lovely, but there are a few things I need from the shops, so you must excuse me.'

She was gabbling, she just knew it, yet somehow she was powerless to stop the frantic flow of words. She stood up, anxious to leave as fast as possible.

'Chrissie, look at me.'

His voice was gentle, yet edged with a firmness which made her obey instantly.

'There's no need to be frightened; it's coffee I'm offering, nothing else. So please, will you stay?'

How could she refuse without making herself look even more foolish? Face flushed with embarrassment that he could read her thoughts so easily, she nodded, then walked hurriedly through to the lounge, needing a few minutes alone to re-gather her composure. She'd always been so in control before, able to cope with any sort of situation, so why did this man send her into a panic?

Too restless and on edge to sit, she paced round the room, picking up a small china figurine, a heavy glass paperweight filled with tiny star-like flowers, then put them back down with scarcely a glance. Tall bookcases flanked either side of the marble fireplace, and she slowly ran a finger along the spines of the books, feeling the brush of paper, cloth and leather rub against her skin. The books were neatly arranged along the shelves, but in no particular order: thrillers next to hefty law books, poetry next to westerns—a catholic collection. She pulled out a thick, glossy travel book and flicked through the pages, still too worried to do more than merely glance at the pictures.

Could she trust him, believe that the only thing on his mind at the moment was coffee? He'd seemed sincere enough, but then she only had to think of Kate to know how good he could be at deception. Was she being foolish letting a few gentle words influence her?

More unsettled than ever, she slid the book back into place, then pulled out a slim volume of poetry, hoping to find some soothing words within its covers. It was a collection of John Donne's sonnets, the pages soft and well-thumbed, as though someone had turned them time after time reading the hauntingly beautiful lines. Had it been Jackson Knight? Did this man, who dealt in death, read love poetry in his spare time?

Based against her previously conceived view of him, the idea should have been ridiculous, but it wasn't. He was a man of so many different facets that it was impossible to place him neatly into any clear category, to make a judgement about him and stick to it. The only predictable thing about him was that he was totally unpredictable!

With a wry smile she pushed the book back, making room for it between a beautifully tooled leatherbound volume and a dilapidated photograph album. Almost unconsciously her hand lingered against the album, a sudden urge to see its contents rising inside her. It seemed such an invasion of privacy, but so tempting that she just couldn't resist. With guilty haste she pulled it out and flicked through the pages, studying the faded snaps of a couple and two young boys. Page by page and year by year the couple aged and the children grew, but not once did Chrissie have any difficulty in picking Jackson out. There was the same harshness even then to the childish features, the same way of staring straight into the camera as though ready to meet everything head on, which singled him out.

The second boy was obviously younger, slimmer built, fair-complexioned, and bore a striking resemblance to the woman, his mother. What had it been like living in that family, believing, if even mistakenly, that he wasn't loved and wanted as much as his younger brother? Had it been enough to make Jackson want to take everything he could from life with no regard for whom it hurt?

Annoyed with herself for finding excuses for him, she snapped the album shut. She didn't want to feel anything for him but hatred. Hands shaking, she tried to force it back into place, murmuring crossly as the ragged cover caught against the edge of the shelf and it fell from her grasp. Anxious to get it out of sight before he appeared, she snatched it up, pausing as a thin sheet of paper fluttered free from the loosened pages. It looked like part of a letter, and curiously

she picked it up, staring down at the flowing script
for a few seconds . . . then felt her blood run cold.
There was a sudden roaring sound in her ears and
she clutched the edge of the shelf to stop herself
falling, breathing slowly and deeply as she fought
to keep the faintness at bay. With painful slowness
the darkness receded, and she stared once more at
the writing, writing which was as familiar as her
own.

'Darling J.
I can hardly wait for Monday to arrive when
we'll be together; it will be like a dream come
true. Of course I can collect the ticket myself,
and yes, I have checked that both my passport
and visa are in order, so don't worry, there
won't be any hitches!
I won't mention to anyone the package you
want me to bring back. I just think it's lovely of
you to go to so much trouble to help out a
friend. I'll take a taxi from the airport and
should see you . . .'

The letter ended there and, desperate to read the
rest of it, Chrissie fanned the pages of the album,
but nothing else fell out. For a long moment she
stared down at the single sheet, her hands
trembling. It was what she'd hoped for, proof that
Jackson Knight was involved in the whole sorry
business, though she doubted if it would stand up
as evidence in a court of law when there wasn't
even a signature on it.
She should have felt pleased by the discovery,
glad that she now had something tangible to go on,

so why did she feel so empty and achingly hollow, as though something vital inside her had just died?

CHAPTER FIVE

CHRISSIE stayed at the flat barely ten minutes longer, drinking scalding hot the coffee he'd made, then leaving, uncaring if he found her abrupt departure strange. Maybe he would put it down to a return of her earlier fears, maybe not; frankly she didn't care what he thought right at that moment. All she knew was that she had to get out of the place before she gave in to the almost overwhelming urge to beat her fists against his chest and make him tell her why he'd done it, why he'd used Kate that way.

With no real idea where she was going, she walked down the street feeling the sun burn through her jacket, but nothing seemed to be able to warm the chill from her body. She felt numb, rigid with a cold which stemmed from the shock of finding that letter. She pushed her hand into her skirt pocket, feeling the crumpled scrap of paper grate against her fingers. She'd barely had time to tuck it out of sight before he came in with the coffee, but there had been no way she could have left it behind. She needed this pathetic little letter as a talisman, a reminder of why she was here, because somehow she seemed to be in danger of losing sight of it.

She crossed the road, ignoring the cacophony of horns as she stepped off the pavement with barely a glance at the traffic. There was a small park on the other side of the street, an oasis of greenery railed off from the pavement, and, slowing her pace, Chrissie walked round till she found the entrance to it. It was almost deserted at this time of the day, just an elderly woman walking an arthritic poodle on a thin leather lead and a young woman pushing a small boy on a rusting swing, and Chrissie sat down on one of the scarred wooden benches, tilting her face to the sun. A shiver ran through her and she clutched her arms tightly round her body, feeling more alone than she'd ever been before in the whole of her life. She felt totally and utterly bereft, but why? Why should the discovery of that note have affected her this way?

She opened her eyes and stared across the park, watching the shifting patterns of light flickering on the dusty city grass. Her thoughts were like that light: flickering, dancing, moving from one thing to another, but she had to make them stop, had to get everything straight in her head or she would never be able to cope. Time was too precious, too short to waste; she had to take a long, hard look at herself, lay bare her feelings and deal ruthlessly with them now.

She felt hurt, let down, but why? All that letter had done was confirm what she'd already suspected, so why should she feel so upset about it? Had she, somewhere deep inside, been nursing a secret hope that she'd been wrong, that Jackson Knight wasn't involved, after all? If she had, then it had been just foolish madness. She'd known the score right from the beginning, made her plans and set about them with a cold determination, and that must be how she continued. Jackson Knight was guilty; it was a fact and the only one that mattered.

The child on the swing was shouting now, shrill, excited cries of pleasure as he swung higher and higher, and Chrissie turned to watch him, a grim, tight smile curving her lips. It was such an ordinary scene: a mother and a child happy in each other's company, a scene that one day should be Kate's. But what chance would Kate ever have of leading a normal life if she was sent to prison? None, absolutely none. No matter how much it hurt, Chrissie knew she had to give her sister back that chance. It was Jackson Knight or Kate . . . there was no choice to make.

There was nothing subtle about the costume she had chosen for that night's performance, far from it! It was the embodiment of blatant sexuality, and Chrissie grinned as she shot one last glance in the mirror. Cut along the lines of a man's tail-suit, the tight black jacket emphasised every luscious curve of her body. Under the jacket she wore a low-cut, silver waistcoat, its deep V-neckline offering tantalising glimpses of the curve of her breasts. There were no trousers to the suit, just high-cut, black satin briefs over fishnet tights which made her legs look incredibly long and shapely. High, black satin pumps, top hat and cane completed the outfit, an outfit which Chrissie knew from experience had set many a male heart thumping. Hopefully it would have the same effect on Jackson Knight!

After she'd returned to the club she'd sat down and methodically gone through all the new facts she'd found out about him, but strangely there had seemed little more to go on. Even that instinctive feeling she'd had about his relationship with his brother had offered nothing useful, not when she still had no idea what had caused the rift between them. No, she was still exactly where she'd been yesterday and the day before and the day before that: certain that he was guilty, yet with no idea how to prove it. What she needed was evidence, strong, indisputable evidence which would stand up in court, and after finding that section of letter she was now more hopeful of getting it. If he'd been careless enough to keep that, then what else might there be lying around? It was imperative that she got another look round his office and the flat, though heaven knew, the idea was daunting. He was nobody's fool, but if she could just throw him off balance, allay any suspicions he might have by using her appearance, then she might just succeed.

'Five minutes, Miss Lane.'

One of the stage-hands rapped on the door to warn her it was nearly time to go on, and Chrissie turned away from the mirror, feeling her insides tighten in sudden apprehension. First nights were always nerve-racking, but now there was more resting on this performance than ever!

She left the dressing-room and made her way quietly to the side of the stage, picking a careful path through the clutter. There was a singer on at the moment, a young girl with a clear, sweet voice, and Chrissie stood in the wings, listening to her.

Through a crack in the curtains she could see the audience seated at their tables, and instinctively her eyes swept over them, picking out any likely victims for later. Several of the tricks she intended to perform demanded audience participation, and she had always found it helpful to get some idea of who might be a likely candidate. The last thing she needed was to get some troublemaker up on the stage.

Her eyes roved slowly round the audience, picking out a middle-aged man just left of centre and a young girl, barely out of her teens, sitting with an older woman at a side table. Next to them was a noisy group of men, and Chrissie made a mental note to avoid looking in their direction when she made her choice. Her gaze moved on, a frisson of surprise racing through her as she spotted Jackson Knight seated at one of the front tables. She hadn't realised he would join the audience for the show, imagining that he would view it from the wings as he'd done at rehearsal.

Dressed in black dinner suit and snowy linen, he looked so devastating that for several seconds Chrissie just stared at him, aching inside with a nameless feeling of regret. Then a movement at his side drew her attention, and for the first time she noticed that he wasn't alone. There was a woman with him, a stunning brunette, and Chrissie felt a flash of quite unreasoning annoyance spear through her. One woman at lunch and another for dinner . . . not bad going by anyone's standards!

As she watched, the woman leant over to whisper something to him, her lips almost brushing his ear. He laughed, tilting his head down to give her his full attention, and in that instant Chrissie knew it couldn't continue. Oh, there was nothing personal in her feelings towards the woman, of course not, just cold, clear logic: if he was giving undivided attention to her, then there was no way he could give that attention to Chrissie—and that would never do. She had to separate them at all costs. She'd gone to a lot of trouble tonight to make herself look alluring, and there was no way she was going to waste all that effort. Thinking quickly, she edged her way round the back of the stage to where Mac was working, and tapped him gently on the shoulder. He swung round, his leathery face splitting into a wide grin as he saw her, then pursing his lips up into a mock whistle of admiration.

'That's some outfit, lass. I reckon you're going to knock them for six tonight in that.'

'I hope so,' she muttered fervently. She took a deep breath, realising she was taking a chance by involving Mac, yet knowing also that she couldn't afford not to. 'Listen, Mac, d'you know who that woman is with Jack?' She deliberately used the shortened form of his name, rolling it familiarly off her tongue as she remembered what he'd said about his closest friends calling him that. She had to give the impression that she was, at the very least, on the way to being classed as one of them.

'Aye, I do that. Marissa Morgan's her name. Her father's that property tycoon who bought up half the city last month. Remember?'

'Yes,' she muttered, her heart sinking. Why on

earth couldn't the woman have been some little
secretary or shop assistant? Why did she have to be
not only beautiful but rich into the bargain? Just
her luck!

'Why do you want to know?'

Mac was watching her keenly, and Chrissie made
an effort to swallow down her disappointment.
Everything now hinged on her acting ability; please
heaven it wouldn't let her down. Lowering her
lashes she stared down at her hands and said softly,
'Well, it's just that I had hoped Jack would watch
my act tonight, but now that Miss Morgan's
here . . . well . . .' She hesitated, as though shy of
continuing.

'You think he won't pay much attention to you,
is that it, lassie?'

'Yes,' she whispered, her voice soft and
tremulous. Glancing up, she could see the
indecision which crossed his face, and held her
breath, waiting to see if he'd take the bait she'd
thrown him.

'Seems to me you really like Jack, then, do you?'

She nodded, unable even at this desperate
moment to push a definite 'yes' from between her
lips. Liking wasn't quite the word to describe her
feelings for Jackson Knight!

'Well, I doubt if you could choose anyone better
to set your cap at, Chrissie. He's a fine man and
there's no mistaking. Frankly I've a feeling you
could be good for him, better than that cold-
hearted young woman.'

'You don't like her, then?' Chrissie asked,
surprised at the venom in his soft voice. Even

though she'd known Mac such a short time, she'd soon realised that kindness was an innate part of him, hidden behind a gruff exterior.

'No, I don't. She used to come to the club a lot when Jonathan was here, then when he left she transferred her attention to Jack, but there's something about her I can't take to. You leave it to me, lass, I'll see she's out of the way when you go on.'

'Thanks, Mac, I owe you one for this.' She leant forwards to press a swift kiss to his lined cheek before hurrying back round the stage.

The singer was reaching her finale now, the clear notes soaring upwards, and Chrissie felt her hopes rising with the music. She chuckled softly. She was going to get his attention all right . . . and keep it for the rest of the evening!

'Ladies and gentlemen, Miss Christina Lane!'

The drums rolled and Chrissie swept on to the stage, smiling round at the audience. With a practised ease she moved into her first trick, a simple affair of pulling a stream of coloured scarves from the tiny pocket of her waistcoat, and hid a smile as she noticed several of the men resume their places. They had been on the point of leaving to go to the gaming-tables, but one glance at her in the stunning costume and they had evidently changed their minds. She shot a quick glance at the front table, and was a trifle disconcerted to see the woman still sitting there, her hand resting on Jackson's sleeve. Close to, she was even more beautiful than Chrissie had realised, with delicate

features and thick, shining hair curling round her
elfin face, and Chrissie desperately prayed that
Mac wouldn't let her down. Marissa Morgan was
competition with a capital C!

The last scarf slithered from her pocket, and she
screwed it up, twisting it deftly between her fingers;
then she opened her hands and out flew a graceful
white dove. The audience clapped enthusiastically
and she bowed low before turning away to settle
the bird on its perch at the back of the stage. When
she turned back, Marissa Morgan was making her
way through the tables, following one of the white-
coated waiters, and Knight was alone at the table.
So Mac had kept his promise, given her the chance,
and there was no way she was going to waste a
second of it.

With an easy skill she went through each stage of
her act, her movements fluid, unhurried, graceful,
aware that the audience was with her every step of
the way. Several times she glanced down at Knight,
and each time he was watching her, his dark eyes
intent. She smiled, a fierce elation rising inside her;
she was going to give him a performance he would
remember for the rest of his life!

She stepped to the front of the stage, waiting till
the applause died down before she spoke.

'Now, ladies and gentlemen, I've come to a point
where I need someone to help me, and who better
than your host here at Knights . . . Mr Jackson
Knight.'

With a brilliant smile she swept a hand towards
him, seeing the fleeting hint of surprise which
crossed his face. For a second he hesitated, and

Chrissie said clearly, 'Come along now, Mr Knight, don't be shy. I promise you'll be quite safe in my hands.'

There was an appreciative chuckle from the audience, and with a wry, self-mocking grin he stood up and headed for the stage.

'Fix! It's a rotten fix!'

The shout came clearly across the room and, startled, Chrissie swung round to see where it came from. Her heart sank. The group of rowdy young men she'd spotted earlier were now on their feet, waving and stamping in time to their mocking cries of 'Fix!' and 'Cheat!' One of them, a heavy-set man with light, curly hair and a florid complexion, was already weaving a path through the tables towards the stage, and Chrissie knew she had to act quickly.

'I can assure you, ladies and gentlemen, this is no fix. Mr Knight had no idea he was going to be asked to help tonight.' It was difficult to maintain the smile, but she was too much of a professional to let her composure slip in public. On her way up the ladder she'd worked at many a rowdy club, and soon learned how to handle troublemakers. It just surprised her that Knights, with its impeccable reputation, should have attracted this sort of client. However, dealing with this little uprising was going to put paid to her plans for the moment. She turned to the dark-haired man standing close beside her.

'There'll be trouble if I insist on you helping. We'd better leave it.'

'Are you sure? Look, Chrissie, I can have them

slung out, just say the word.'

There was a grim look on his face, and Chrissie knew that nothing would give him greater pleasure than having the whole bunch thrown out on their ear. For a second she was tempted, but deep down she knew it was the wrong way to handle the incident. At the moment the men were just noisy and rowdy, but it would need very little to tip them over the edge to violence. Even now the girl and the woman on the next table to them were looking worried. If she asked him to have them thrown out, then there was no telling who could get hurt. She might want her first performance to be memorable, but not because she'd instigated some sort of brawl!

'I'm sure. It will be all right.'

He nodded and sat back down at the table, his fist clenched on the white cloth as though he was holding on to his temper with effort.

The man had arrived at the stage now and stood at the bottom of the steps, swaying. Chrissie turned to him, her voice filled with a light irony which wasn't missed by the audience.

'Well, it's nice of you to offer to help, Mr . . .'

'Colin,' he muttered, his voice thick and slurred. 'And I'll be glad to help you any time, darling.'

His eyes slid over her, hot and greedy, so that she was filled with sudden revulsion. Glancing away, she could see the spasm of rage which contorted Jackson's face, and realised it would take very little for him to carry out his earlier threat. She summoned up every tiny shred of composure she possessed, determined that the man wasn't going to ruin her first performance.

'Right then, Colin. Come up here and I'll tell you what I want you to do.'

She led him across the stage, settling him down at one side of the table before moving to sit behind it. The trick she intended to do was basically very simple, but appeared difficult to the audience. From out of a pack of cards she would find the cards he would select and mark with a felt-tipped pen. However, at no point in the proceedings would she ever see what the cards were until she drew them from the pack. It was a trick which she'd spent hours perfecting over the years, but one which always went down well.

She ran quickly through the instructions with him, pleased to find that he wasn't too intoxicated to follow her meaning. Then, with skilful dexterity she shuffled the cards, her hands faltering slightly as she felt something skim up her leg. She glanced down and for a second stayed transfixed with horror. Under cover of the silk cloth the man was fondling her leg, his hot, damp hand moving familiarly up her thigh. Suddenly Chrissie was filled brimfull with a furious rage. How dared he? How dared he touch her? Leaning forwards, her lips curved into a tiny false smile for the benefit of the audience, she murmured softly, 'If you don't get your hand off me, you're going to be sorry.'

'Who are you trying to kid, darling? You're loving every minute of it.'

His hand moved higher and Chrissie knew she had to act. Maybe he thought she wouldn't do anything in front of the audience, but was he in for a shock!

Reaching out, she pretended to pluck a coin first from behind his left ear, then from behind his right, her hand moving back and forth with a dizzying speed so that coins seemingly rained from the air behind his head. The audience loved it, thinking it was part of the act, and clapped loudly, which was exactly what she'd intended. Under cover of the applause she dropped her hand a fraction, digging her nails hard into the soft flesh behind his ear. He gasped with pain, jerking sharply back so that his hand fell away from her leg. His face suffused with an ugly colour, and just for an instant Chrissie felt a flicker of real alarm race through her.

'Why, you little——' he began, but she didn't allow him to finish.

'Forget it,' she snapped, her voice no more than an icy whisper, covered by the sound of the clapping. 'There's a man down there who'll take great pleasure in sorting you out, so let's just get on with the trick, shall we, and call it quits?'

He followed her gaze, blanching as he caught sight of the expression on Jackson Knight's face. Reassured that he would give no further trouble, Chrissie led him through the rest of the trick, barely giving him time to think. When it was over she escorted him from the stage, watching with a false smile of gratitude as he made his way back to his table. Once or twice she'd had trouble with various so-called helpers, but never anything which had been so distasteful!

Three minutes later her act was over, and limp

with relief, Chrissie bowed to the audience. From out of the corner of her eye she could see Jackson and two of the security guards escorting the group from the room with a quiet, ruthless efficiency. It had been a nasty experience, but thankfully it seemed to be over. With one last bow she swept from the stage and hurried back to the dressing-room, closing the door firmly behind her. Her hands were shaking, her knees trembling so much that she just had to sit down. Closing her eyes, she willed herself to be calm, but it was impossible when she could still feel the loathsome touch of that hand sliding up her skin. She shuddered, sickness welling hotly inside her at the memory.

The door opened abruptly and she spun round in sudden fear, wondering if the man had somehow followed her.

'Are you all right?'

Closing the door behind him, Jackson stepped into the room, a grim tightness compressing his mouth as he took in her frightened expression. She nodded, trying to force her lips into some semblance of a smile, but they refused to obey. In a giant surge, all that had happened that day suddenly caught up with her and she felt her eyes fill with tears. That, on top of everything else, had been the absolute and final straw. She glanced down, desperate to avoid his gaze, but he'd already seen the silver glitter on her lashes.

'Don't, sweetheart; don't cry.'

Hunching down on his heels, he tilted her face, gently brushing the tears from her cheeks. His face was filled with so much tenderness and concern that Chrissie, in her overwrought state, cried all the harder. It wasn't fair that this one man who was trying to offer consolation was the one man she couldn't accept it from.

'Oh, Chrissie, my love, don't.'

He reached out, pulling her unresisting body hard against him, and held her tightly, so tightly that she could feel the heavy beat of his heart against her breast. Gently he ran his hand over her hair, his fingers stroking and soothing while he murmured a stream of barely heard endearments.

They stayed like that for several minutes, her face pressed against the hard ridge of his shoulder, his hand stroking her hair, and gradually a feeling of peace stole over her. It felt so good to be close to him, to feel the hard warmth of his body, the steady, reassuring beat of his pulse, that she never wanted it to end. She was tired of struggling, tired of having to cope with everything, tired of always having to be strong. Just for once it was wonderful to give in to weakness and let someone else do the caring.

'When I realised what he was doing, I could have killed him for it, do you know that? Killed him with my bare hands!'

There was violence in his voice now, a real, live violence which cut through the feeling of contentment, destroying it completely. With a shiver she pulled away, rubbing a hand over her wet face, feeling the coldness of reality close round her. What was she doing? How could she have forgotten so quickly just who he was and what he'd done? Was she really so spineless that it took only a few soft words, a tender gesture, to make her forget?

Filled with self-disgust, she plucked a handful of tissues from the box on the dressing-table and scrubbed at the mascara patches under her eyes, wishing she could wipe away the memory of those brief moments in his arms as easily.

'Are you quite sure you're all right?'

'Yes, I'm fine, really. I'm sorry about all that, I . . .'

'Forget it, Chrissie, it's understandable. I'm only sorry that you were subjected to that on your first night here.'

He stood up, thrusting his hands deep into his trouser pockets as though it was the only way he could stop himself from hitting something. 'We don't usually have trouble here—oh, the odd over-enthusiastic reveller, but never much more. I employ staff to check on who comes in this place, and when I find out who let that group in there'll be trouble, believe me.'

There was a grimness to his deep voice which boded ill for the person concerned, and Chrissie thanked heaven it wasn't her. Crossing Jackson Knight would be quite an experience, one she hoped she wouldn't have to face—at least, not at the moment. With a shaking hand she pulled another wad of tissues from the box and creamed the rest of the make-up from her face, casting a wry glance at her pale complexion. It was hard to believe that a mere half-hour ago she'd been sitting here looking the very picture of allure; now she looked about as alluring as a ghost!

'By the way, I enjoyed that little trick you pulled.'

'What do you mean?' she asked, surprised at the note of amusement now in his voice.

'That little sleight of hand with the nails into that guy's neck; now, where did you learn that sort of thing, I wonder?'

She grinned, the tension suddenly leaving her body. 'Oh, here and there. A girl always needs a trick or two up her sleeve, you know.'

He laughed. 'Well, that was probably one of your best efforts. But seriously, Chrissie, how often do you have to deal with incidents like that?'

'Not very often now, thankfully. A few years back, when I was just getting established, I worked some of the rougher clubs, and things could get kind of awkward at times, but I soon learned to cope. You have to, as any performer will tell you, if you want to survive. Mind you, the children's parties I do are sometimes tricky.'

'Children's parties?' he echoed blankly.

'Yes. Believe me, when you have twenty or so of the little dears all clustering round trying to see how everything works, then things can get difficult. It's not unknown for me to go home with a few bruises after one of them.'

'Really? Sounds like a dangerous business you're in, then.' Leaning back against the wall, he smiled at her, the harshness gone from his face, and she smiled back.

'Oh, it is. I'm seriously thinking about getting a "minder", you know, especially for the under-fives parties. They're the worst!'

'How about if I applied for the job? D'you think I'd be suitable?'

Suddenly all the laughter left his face, and Chrissie knew with instinctive certainty that it was now or never. Her answer would tip the balance of their relationship one way or the other. She hesitated for the briefest moment as fear of what would happen rose up inside her. Then, filled with a strange feeling of the inevitable, she whispered softly, 'Yes . . . yes, I think you'd be very suitable.'

He went quite still, his body rigid with tension, and Chrissie felt her heart begin to hammer with a heavy, sickening thud. She looked down, swallowing hard, wondering if she'd been mad to issue that blatant invitation.

'Second thoughts already, Chrissie?' he asked gently and she glanced up at him through her lashes, wondering what he meant, but there was nothing on his face which gave her any idea.

'What do you mean?' she asked at last, unable to bear a second longer the silence which filled the room.

'Just that it seems like some sort of ritual: two steps forward and three back. When are you going to start running towards me and stop running back?'

'Is that what you think I've been doing?'

'You know it is. Advance and retreat—but why? That's what puzzles me. I know you're attracted to me the same as I am to you, yet there's something holding you back. What is it, Chrissie? What are you really afraid of?'

You . . . the answer rang through her head, but

she knew there was no way she could say it. There was no way she could explain that the only thing which frightened her was the man himself. Suddenly the desire to blurt out the whole sorry story, to lay the facts before him and make him explain, was so great that she had to bite her lip to stop the words from escaping. There was no way she could risk doing that, no way she could expect him to admit what he'd done. It was his secret and hers; the one thing which linked them together, yet at the same time drove them apart.

'Well, Chrissie?'

It was obvious that he expected an answer, and her mind raced as she tried to find something convincing, something which would explain the strange way she'd been acting. He was right, of course, she had been giving him all green lights, then as soon as he looked like advancing she had turned them hastily to red! Frantically her mind raced round, searching for something, and finally she came up with an excuse so old she could almost hear it creaking with fatigue!

'I just need time, Jack, some time to absorb everything that's happened. It's all been so sudden that I can't believe what I'm feeling is real.'

'And that's just it is it . . . time?'

She nodded, not daring to speak in case he detected the note of untruth in her voice.

'Well, if that's what you want, then it's yours, as much time as you need; but be warned, Chrissie. One day you're going to come running towards me and I'll catch you and never let you go again.'

With a gentle smile he left the room, closing the

door softly behind him. Chrissie stared after him,
wondering how much time she had till he kept that
promise.

CHAPTER SIX

IT WAS raining, heavy, fat drops falling steadily from the black night sky, and Chrissie, standing just inside the doorway to the club, grimaced. She turned up the collar of the coral jacket, huddling down into the meagre protection it offered, and rued the fact that she'd not thought to bring an umbrella.

'Filthy night, isn't it?'

She turned to smile at Mac, who had come up behind her, an old worn parka zipped tightly round his neck.

'It certainly is. I was just wishing I'd thought to bring an umbrella with me, but it was so nice when I set out this morning that it didn't seem necessary. I should have known better; when can you ever trust English weather?'

With a small wry grin she stepped out into the street, feeling the cold rain sting against her hot cheeks. It was almost two a.m. and she was tired beyond belief. The second performance of the cabaret, scheduled for midnight, had run late, so that it had been way after one o'clock before she'd gone on to an enthusiastic reception. There had been no doubt that her act had been a success, but at the moment Chrissie felt too drained to draw even the tiniest bit of pleasure from the fact. All she wanted to do now was get herself home to bed and sleep for the next twelve hours solid, and then some!

'How are you getting back home?'

Mac stood beside her, the hood of the coat pulled up over his head to protect him from the downpour, and Chrissie paused for a second, brushing a rivulet of rain from her cheek.

'Oh, I'll get a taxi. There's a taxi rank down the road, isn't there?'

She pointed down the road, and Mac nodded, a faintly troubled expression on his face.

'Yes, there is, but I don't like the idea of you walking down there on your own. You don't know who's about at this time of the morning.'

'I'll be fine, Mac, don't worry. See you tomorrow.'

With a small wave she turned and hurried down the quiet street, her high heels clicking sharply against the pavement. A nasty little wind had blown up, scurrying the cold drops of rain straight into her face, and she bent her head against the onslaught. Her jacket was thin linen, and within minutes she could feel dampness penetrating right through to her skin. Clamping her bag tightly to her side, she quickened her pace, praying there would be a cab free when she got there. Frankly, the idea of hanging around in this deluge waiting for one to come back in was far from appealing.

'Remember me, sweetheart?'

The man stepped out of the alleyway, blocking her path, and she stopped dead, her stomach lurching with shock. She raised her hand, wiping the rain from her eyes as she stared at him, fear rising inside her as she recognised the heavy-set features and florid complexion. It was the man from the club, her so-called helper; what had he said his name was? That was it, Colin. But what did he want? A spiralling tightness curled in the pit of her stomach as she realised she already had a pretty good idea, but there was no way she could let him see her fear.

'What do you want?' she demanded, desperately trying to keep her voice steady while inside every tiny bit of her was shaking.

'Want? Well, I would have thought that was obvious. Did you really think you could get away with it, you little bitch?'

Even in the semi-darkness Chrissie could see the look of hatred on his face, and slowly she took a careful step backwards. The street was deserted—no cars, no pedestrians, nobody to help her if he turned nasty, and she had the horrible suspicion that getting nasty was his main intention. Slowly, carefully, she eased her bag round, taking a firmer grip on the strap. If he took one step, just one towards her, then so help her, she would hit him with it!

'Get out of my way,' she ordered, her voice filled with an icy scorn.

He laughed, a horrible, jarring sound which made the fear rolling coldly through her race to the very tips of her toes.

'Make me, darling. Come on, use one of your little tricks and make me. I'm sure I would enjoy it.'

He leered at her, his face filled with an

expression which made her feel sick to her stomach with revulsion, a revulsion heightened by the memory of how it had felt to have his hand on her skin. She prayed that he wouldn't get the chance to repeat the action!

She eyed him warily, weighing up her chances of rushing past him, but frankly they seemed pretty slim. He was standing slap-bang in the middle of the pavement, his hands clenched loosely at his sides. No matter which side she chose, he could easily catch her.

'Come on, then, darling, try it.'

It was obvious that he'd read her intention, and Chrissie swallowed hard, trying to quell the rising surge of panic. If there was no way past him, then her only hope lay in getting back to the club. She took another step backwards, her heart thumping painfully as he took one step forwards, keeping the same pitifully small amount of distance between them. Desperately she tried to remember just how far it was to the club: one hundred yards, two, three? Was there just the smallest chance that she could reach it before he caught her? It was worth a try.

Spinning on her heels, she went to run back up the street, pain shooting hotly up her arm as he caught hold of the strap of her bag and wrenched her back.

'Oh, no, you don't. You don't get away that easily.'

Hatred and a strange, terrifying excitement shone in his pale eyes, and Chrissie knew that she'd reached the last of her options. She pulled the bag free, swinging it wildly at his head, missing him by inches.

'Why, you . . .!'

'Chrissie!'

The shout came from behind her and she jumped, shooting a startled glance over her shoulder, and she felt her knees go weak with relief as she recognised Jackson Knight running down the road towards them. It was obvious that the man had recognised him, too, for with a foul oath he pushed past her, shoving her aside with such force that she fell to the pavement, banging her shoulder painfully against the cold, wet flags. For a few seconds she lay there, feeling stunned. It had all been so quick, so sudden—one minute he was there, the next he'd gone—that it was hard to believe it had really happened. Only the throbbing ache in her arm and shoulder bore testimony to the fact that it had been very real.

'Chrissie, are you all right?' With a total disregard for the slushy pavement, Jack knelt beside her, his hands running gently down her body as he felt for broken bones, and she forced a weak, tremulous smile to her shaking lips.

'Yes, I'm fine, or I will be when I get up out of this puddle.'

'Here, let me help you.'

He stood up, helping her to her feet with a gentle concern which seemed at variance with the grim expression on his face as he stared after the fleeing figure.

'If I ever get my hands on him . . .' His voice was like black ice, filled with rage, and Chrissie shivered, hating to hear such a bitter note. She reached out, laying her hand gently on his arm, feeling the fine tremor which raced through the hard muscles.

'Leave it, Jack,' she said softly. 'I doubt if he'll ever try it again. Frankly, I think you scared him almost as much as he scared me.'

It was difficult to make a joke out of her recent terror, but instinct told her it was the only way to cope with it. If she really allowed herself to think what could have happened if he hadn't appeared, then she had the feeling she would just keel over. She shuddered, long, trembling spasms which tore at her slender body, rippling through her and into the man who was holding her. He gazed into her face, his eyes dark, still tainted with anger and a strange, tiny glimmer of fear which surprised her. Had he been afraid . . . for her? Suddenly the idea was strangely unsettling and she drew away, bending to retrieve her bag from the pavement. That this hard, tough man should have been afraid for her was something she would have to come to terms with, for somehow it added a new depth to their relationship which she wasn't prepared for.

'Come along.' He took her firmly by the arm and headed back up the street.

'Where are you taking me?' she asked, automatically following his lead.

'To the flat, of course.'

'Oh, but you can't do that! I mean, I've got to get home. It's late and . . .'

'Shut up, Chrissie, will you? Just for once in your life, shut up and let someone do something for you.'

'What do you mean?' she demanded, taking an
instant dislike to the tone of his deep voice.

'What do I mean?'

He stopped and swung her round, holding her in
front of him, his long, hard fingers biting deep into
the soft flesh of her upper arms. In the light of an
overhead streetlamp, his face was devoid of any
colour, a harsh, stern mask of angles and shadows.
Only his eyes seemed alive, glittering like jet. Rain
was pouring down, streaming over his head,
flattening his dark hair to his skull, but he seemed
oblivious to it as he stared at her.

'I mean that no one but an idiot would have
gone walking about alone at this time of night. I
couldn't believe it when Mac came back in and told
me. Why the hell didn't you tell me you had no way
of getting home, eh?' He shook her so hard that
her head lolled back and forth on her slender neck.
'Well, damn it, woman, why didn't you?'

'I . . . I thought I'd get a taxi. Anyway, what
business is it of yours how I get home? You might
employ me, Mr Knight, but you don't own me!'

Filled with a sudden burning anger, equal to his,
she tried to pull away, twisting and turning in his
grasp like a wild animal in a trap. How dared he
talk to her like this? Just who did he think he was?
Desperately she pulled at his restraining hold, but
he wouldn't let her go, his hands fastening tighter
round her arms so that she had to make a conscious
effort not to cry out at the pain he was inflicting.

'So that's it, is it? I don't own you. Well, we'll
see about that, lady. We'll see!'

With a sudden wrench he dragged her against him so hard that the breath whooshed from her body; then, bending his head, he fastened his mouth to hers in a fierce almost brutal kiss. Desperately she tried to move her head, tried to turn her face away, but he clamped his hand round the back of her neck so that she was powerless to move. His strength was immense and, even if she hadn't been feeling so weak and shaky, Chrissie doubted if she could have broken free. Standing rigid, she suffered the punishing kiss, anger and a fierce hatred burning inside her. She hated him, hated him to the very depths of her soul!

Tears gathered in her eyes, trickling down her cheeks to mingle saltily with the clear, sweet rain and run across their joined lips. Chrissie could taste the saltiness, knew he must taste it too, but she was powerless to stop the tears. The pressure of his lips eased slightly, then slowly he drew back, his eyes black as they stared at her pale, set face. With a low groan he gathered her to him, holding her against his chest as he rocked her gently, as though offering comfort to a frightened child.

'Oh, Chrissie, I'm sorry, so sorry. I didn't mean to do that, believe me. It just came from nowhere.'

'It's all right.' Standing stiff and aloof in his arms, Chrissie blinked to chase the betraying tears away. She wanted nothing from this man, nothing . . . not apologies, not comfort, nothing.

'It's not all right,' he said softly, his lips close to her ear. 'I frightened you then almost as much as he did, and there can be no excuse for that.'

A wealth of self-disgust laced his voice, and

unwillingly she felt herself softening. He'd been angry, frightened by what could have happened to her, so it was probably natural that he would react in such a way when she deliberately provoked him.

'Jack . . .'

'Chrissie . . .'

Both turned and spoke at the same moment, a strange stillness settling over them as their lips met in a wholly unintentional contact. For a second they stood quite still, lips just touching, then gently, carefully, he turned his head a fraction more till his mouth settled fully over hers. He paused, his body rigid, and Chrissie knew with instinctive certainty that she only had to move and he would let her go without a struggle. The strange thing was that she no longer wanted to. Suddenly all the fear, all the hatred, had gone, burning itself up into one great flare of passion which could no longer be denied. She wanted his kiss, wanted it more than she'd ever wanted anything in the whole of her life.

With a low, almost despairing moan, she moved her mouth under his, her lips clinging, teasing, inciting his to respond. Cold rain spilled over their faces, soaked their clothes, but neither felt it, locked in a world which was warmed and lit by the fire of passion.

The kiss ran on and on, then slowly he drew back, his fingers tracing a delicate path down her wet cheek, as though he couldn't quite bear to break all contact. Gently he rubbed his thumb over her lips, and Chrissie closed her eyes as she felt a tingling echo of awareness race through her body.

Deep down, she knew it was wrong, knew that she should never have allowed that kiss to happen, but there was no way she could ever regret it. How could she regret something which had felt so right and been so devastatingly perfect?

'Will you come back to the flat with me, Chrissie?'

His voice was oddly hesitant, as though he was almost afraid to ask the question; yet there was no hesitation in her answer.

'Yes. I'll come.'

He smiled, holding out his hand, and slowly she linked her fingers with his, knowing that what she did now had no bearing whatsoever on her need to help Kate. This was purely and simply for herself.

Half an hour later, seated at the dressing-table, towelling her damp hair, Chrissie paused to study her reflection as though she was suddenly seeing the face of a stranger. Through the door leading to the bathroom she could hear the steady splashing of the shower running as Jack took his turn to wash the mud and rain from his body. She had already showered, and now, snugly wrapped in a huge terry-cloth robe, was beginning to feel rather nervous. They had spoken little since they came into the flat, he seemingly more concerned that she should get warm and dry before she caught a chill, and she still too wrapped up in the wonder of that kiss to waste time on words. Now, however, Chrissie was starting to wonder just what she was doing. She dropped the towel, studying the bruised softness of her mouth for a long moment, then traced a finger over her lips, shuddering at the memories it evoked.

The shower stopped and, suddenly self-conscious, she picked up a comb to ease the snarls from her long hair, feeling the tension curling deep inside her. Outside in the street, her body alive, heated by passion, it had all seemed so right and natural; she would go back to the flat and what would happen—well, it would just happen. Now, however, with her emotions more under control, nothing seemed as straightforward and simple.

The bathroom door opened and he stepped into the room, a towel slung low round his hips his only covering. For a second Chrissie could only stare at him, her eyes lingering on the hard, muscled width of his chest, the narrow, masculine hips, the long, strong length of his legs, feeling a quaking shudder race through her. She wanted him even now, so help her, wanted him as she'd wanted no man ever before!

'How do you feel now?' Picking up another towel, he rubbed his wet hair, the black silk strands gleaming under the light with the iridescent sheen of a raven's wing. She swallowed, trying to ease the knot of tension from her throat before she spoke.

'Fine, thank you. A lot better than before and a lot cleaner.'

She summoned up a tiny smile, but it was a poor effort by any standards. All at once she'd become aware of the absolute quiet both in the flat and out, the total lack of sound and life, as though they were the only two people left on earth. She glanced down, running her thumbnail sharply against the teeth of the comb, feeling the grating, discordant sound tear through her.

'Chrissie, look at me.'

There was a gentleness to his voice, and slowly she looked up, her eyes not quite able to meet his dark ones. What was she doing here in this room, sharing these intimacies with a virtual stranger? Suddenly she would have given anything she possessed to be a million miles away.

'Have you ever slept with a man before?'

The question startled her so much that she stared at him, colour staining her cheeks in a crimson tide. She shook her head, then whispered, 'No,' as though frightened he might not understand what she meant.

'No . . . I thought not. Why, Chrissie?'

Why? The question rippled round and round her head in circles, and she sat quite still, giving it her full and undivided attention. She supposed it was surprising really, to be a twenty-three-year-old virgin in this day and age. So why hadn't she done what most other girls of her age had? Why had she 'saved herself'? There must be a reason for it.

'Why, Chrissie?' he repeated softly. He crossed the room, standing so close beside her that she could feel the moist heat from his damp body cloud on her skin. 'Tell me, love.'

She looked up, her eyes filled with confusion, wondering what to say, then realising it could be nothing but the truth. If nothing else, she owed him that.

'Because I never wanted anyone,' she answered quietly.

'But you want me?'

'Yes,' she whispered, suddenly unable to deny her feelings. 'Yes, I want you, Jack.'

He closed his eyes, his hands clenching and unclenching at his sides as though he was fighting some hard inward battle for control. When he looked at her again there was such a wealth of tenderness on his face that she felt the breath catch in her throat. All at once her pulse began to hammer, fast, hard little flurries, and heat curled in the pit of her stomach. Maybe, just maybe it wasn't wrong to be here, after all.

'Thank you,' he said, and she shot him a startled look, wondering what he meant.

'What for?'

'For being honest with me, Chrissie, for not trying to cover up something that's so important with lies and falsehoods.'

He turned away, wrenching open the door of one of the tall wardrobes to pull out an armful of blankets and toss them carelessly on to the floor.

'What are you doing?' she asked, staring blankly at the growing heap of bedding. He stopped, resting his head against the edge of the doorframe, and even from that distance she could see the tension in his body.

'Giving you what you asked me for earlier.'

'What I asked you for . . . Jack, what are you talking about?' She stood up, pulling the robe tighter round her body, feeling suddenly cold.

'Time, Chrissie. I said I'd give you time to get used to me, to us, and I've no intention of going back on that promise.' He shouldered the door shut, then turned to face her. 'Look, Chrissie, I know it would be only too easy to take you to bed now, this very night. There's that much feeling racing between us, it would need very little spark to set everything burning, but it's just not right. Deep down you've still got reservations, and there's no way I'm going to take a chance on you regretting what we do by being carried away by the moment. When we make love, Chrissie, that's exactly what it will be, *love*, nothing less. I don't want you waking up tomorrow and regretting it as though it was something to be ashamed of. I want you to come to me willingly, wanting me as much as I want you and free from any regrets. So tonight I'm going to do the only honourable thing and sleep on the sofa. Just thank heavens there's not a lot left of the night.'

With a wry grin he left the room, and Chrissie stared after him, her mind blank of anything except one tiny word . . .'love'. Was that what he really wanted from her?

Sleep was elusive, ebbing and flowing like a high spring tide, so that it was way past dawn before Chrissie finally fell into an uneasy doze. When she awoke, it was midday, the sun was high in the sky and she was alone in the flat.

She slid out of bed, pulling the thick towelling robe on over the lacy camisole and briefs she'd worn to sleep in, then made her way through into the lounge. She stared round, her eyes halting on the neatly folded heap of blankets piled on one of the sofas; mute evidence of where he'd spent the night. For a moment she stood quite still, remembering the sound of his voice, the look in his dark eyes before he'd left her, then shivered as a strange feeling of excitement rose inside her. Love . . . had he meant it? Had he really been saying that he was falling in love with her? She hugged the idea to her for a moment, savouring it, tasting it, exploring the possibility of it with a greedy pleasure. Then slowly the realisation of what she was doing came flooding back.

Love. How could there ever be that between them? Pain stabbed at her heart, tearing through her with an intensity which made her stagger, so that she gripped the back of the sofa, her knuckles turning white. She could never love Jackson Knight, could never allow him to offer love to her. It was a betrayal of everything between her and Kate.

Tears stung at her eyes, and with a shaking hand she brushed them away, knowing she was being foolish to allow such an idea to upset her. What he'd said last night had probably been part of some well-rehearsed act, something he performed when he found the odd, reluctant female in his flat; it was doubtful he'd meant one single word of it. A man like Jackson Knight could never even know what love meant.

With leaden steps she walked back into the bedroom and dragged on her clothes, shuddering at the clammy feel of the damp linen and silk against her skin. Her suit was ruined, stained down one side where she'd fallen to the pavement, the collar limp and curling, the shoulders oddly twisted from its soaking. The best place for it would be the bin when she got home, along with all the other memories of this disastrous night.

She dragged a comb through her hair, then forced her feet into her water-stiffened sandals and glanced round, realising she couldn't just leave without making some effort to tidy the room behind her. The bed was rumpled, the sheets knotted from her constant tossings and turnings, and, suddenly anxious to remove all traces of her occupation, she stripped them from the bed and re-made it with fresh linen from the cupboards. Satisfied that everything was neat and tidy, she picked up her bag and hurried towards the front door, then stopped, her hand resting on the latch as a sudden thought struck her. Here she was, alone in the flat, so why on earth wasn't she making the most of the opportunity to search the place? Heaven knew she might never get such a marvellous chance again. She just couldn't afford to waste it.

It took little more than ten minutes to go through the drawers and cupboards in the bedroom, yet to Chrissie every single one of those minutes felt like a hundred. Her heart was pounding, her hands damp with nervous perspiration as she searched through the neatly arranged stacks of clothing, taking care not to disturb any of them. Finding nothing in the bedroom, she moved into the lounge and worked methodically through the papers in the writing-desk, a deep feeling of distaste rising inside her. It seemed so wrong to be going through his things, to be reading private papers like some common sneak thief, but it had to be done. Steeling herself, she turned her attention to the bookshelves and slowly, deliberately searched through every book on every shelf, determined not to miss anything, yet by the time she had finished she was close to tears. She had never felt so disgusted with herself before in the whole of her life. It was only the thought of Kate, still locked in that prison cell, facing years of a similar existence, which had kept her going.

The telephone rang, the sound unnaturally loud in the silence, and she jumped before turning nervously towards it. Who could it be? Should she answer it? For a few seconds she stood undecided, but there was really no way she could ignore its insistent summons. With a shaking hand she lifted the receiver.

'Chrissie?'

There was no mistaking that deep, soft voice, and Chrissie felt a tremor she just couldn't control run through her as she heard it. Unbidden, an image of how he had looked last night, his body damp from the shower, his eyes dark and tender, rose up, and she closed her eyes, willing it to disappear.

'Are you still there?'

'Yes, of course,' she managed to answer, drawing in a deep, shaky breath.

'Are you all right? You sound strange.'

There was concern in his voice now, and Chrissie realised she had to make the effort to sound natural at all costs. There was no way she wanted him rushing back to the flat to check on her, no way she wanted to see him at the moment, while she was so very vulnerable. All it would need was one swift glance at her face to see the guilt about what she'd been doing plainly written there!

'I'm fine. I've not long got up, so that's probably why I sound funny,' she lied quickly.

'Mmm, little sleepy head.' There was a teasing softness to his tone, and she swallowed hard, summoning up every shred of control she still possessed. She mustn't allow herself to be seduced by those honeyed tones which seemed to offer a taste of heaven. She had to remember what he was really like, that he didn't mean any of it, as Kate had found out to her cost. She bit her lip hard, willing the pain to bring her back to her senses and drive out all those tormenting echoes which lay in her mind. There could be no heaven with Jackson Knight, only a harsh and bitter hell.

'Did you want me for something?' she asked, her voice a fraction more level.

'Not really. I was just checking that you were all right, that's all.'

'Well, I'm fine, thank you; no after-effects from last night, thank heavens.'

'None?' he asked quietly, and instantly she knew what he meant. How should she answer? Should she deny there had been anything between them, as every instinct was demanding, or should she still leave her options open? In a quandary, she stayed silent, hearing him sigh softly at the other end of the line.

'Is it retreat time now, Chrissie? Was I right in what I said last night?'

'What do you mean?'

'That you would have regretted it this morning if we had made love.'

'I don't know,' she whispered, her cheeks flaming.

'Don't you? Well, think about it, then, my love; think about it hard, because one day soon I'm going to ask you again, and there will be no going back on your decision then. I won't let you.'

There was just the tiniest hint of a threat in his voice now which steadied her far faster than anything else could have done. Just who did he think he was, giving her ultimatums? However, before she could think up a sharp answer for him he said shortly, 'Well, I'll see you tonight. Take care, and by the way, Chrissie, if you look in the kitchen you'll find something there for you.'

'Something for me? What? Jack . . . Jack!'

He'd hung up and, puzzled, she hurried through into the kitchen, staring at the long white envelope propped against the kettle. Her name was neatly written on it, yet for several minutes she just looked at it, making no attempt to pick it up. Then, with a shrug at her own foolishness, she ripped it open, tipping the contents on to the long, polished counter-top.

There was a silver key inside and a thin single sheet of paper and, suddenly curious, she smoothed the sheet out to read it.

'Take this key to the flat, Chrissie, and use it any time you ever need shelter from a storm.'

Her lips twisted into a small wry smile as she read

the sentence. 'Shelter from the storm . . .' My
heaven, this was the very eye of the hurricane!

CHAPTER SEVEN

SOME twelve hours later, Chrissie bowed one last time to the audience, then left the stage and hurried through to the dressing-room to change. The second performance of the cabaret was now over and she was free to leave, or would be if she managed to escape from Jackson Knight! Not bothering to remove the heavy stage make-up, she dragged on jeans and sweater, then picked up her bag, a feeling of urgency racing through her.

There had been no sign of Knight when she'd first got back to the club, and a few discreet enquiries had elicited the information that he wasn't expected to be in that night. However, just minutes into the second performance of her act a strange prickling sensation up the back of her neck had made her wonder if that information might be wrong. Under cover of arranging a display of paper flowers which she'd just plucked from an 'empty' vase, she had glanced round, her heart leaping painfully as she had spotted his familiar figure seated at the bar. He had raised his glass to her, a strangely intimate little gesture even across the width of the crowded room, and every one of her senses had shot on to red-alert. Why had he come? What did he want? Simple questions with an equally simple, if disturbing, answer . . . her! He had come in specially to see her, but there was no way she wanted to see him while all the memories of last night were still so vividly and shockingly clear. No, she had to avoid him at all costs till she had all those memories strictly under control.

Her mind in turmoil, she'd gone through the rest of her routine scarcely aware of what she was doing, her every thought focused on just one thing . . . escape. Now it looked as though she might just succeed. She eased the door open and peered out into the passage, breathing a soft sigh of relief when she found it empty. For a few horrible minutes she'd wondered if he would be waiting outside for her, but she'd been mistaken. With stealthy haste she crept out of the room, closing the door quietly behind her.

'Miss Lane!'

One of the stage-hands called her name and she jumped, raising a hand to her throat to stem the sudden, nervous flutter of her pulse.

'Yes?'

'Mr Knight said to tell you that he'll meet you by the front door when you're ready.'

Without waiting for an answer, the boy turned away and Chrissie thought quickly, hastily reviewing her options—not that they were that extensive. She could either go out of the front and meet Jackson Knight, or she could sneak out of the back and avoid him. It wasn't difficult to decide which was the most appealing.

She took to her heels and ran swiftly along the corridors towards the back door, realising she only had a short time till he became suspicious and came looking for her. He mustn't find her . . . not yet!

Last night she'd been lucky; she'd played with fire, yet had avoided getting too badly burnt. However, common sense told her that next time it could be a quite different story. Next time Jackson Knight might not be willing to let her go so readily, nor might she be as eager to make him! She had to get away now, get some time and space to damp down her feelings so there would be no danger of any conflagration in the future.

She'd reached the last corridor now, the narrow one which led out to the back courtyard and, suddenly aware of the painful stitch in her side, Chrissie slowed her pace. She was wearing her trainers again, the soft soles making only the faintest whisper of sound against the bare floor, so there was nothing to warn the couple partly hidden behind a tower of cardboard boxes of her approach. For a second Chrissie didn't know who was the most startled, she or the two women, one of whom was Moira Wade. There was silence, then Moira Wade spoke, her voice filled with an icy anger.

'What are you doing here?'

Chrissie swallowed, suddenly inexplicably frightened. There was something in those cold pale eyes which sent a chill of melting ice trickling down her spine. She glanced away, staring at the second woman for a moment, till she realised with a start of surprise that it was Marissa Morgan. Dressed in a hooded coat which partly shrouded her face as she was, Chrissie hadn't recognised her at first. But what on earth was she doing here in the store-room talking to Moira at this hour?

It was a puzzle, but one Chrissie didn't have time to work out right at the moment. Time was passing and Jackson would be wondering where she'd got to. She had to get out of the club at once, and leave the two women to their plotting in private.

'Sorry if I startled you,' she said clearly. 'But I thought I'd just pop out the back way.'

She summoned up her coolest smile and walked past them, a tiny flutter of alarm tingling inside her as she noticed how Moira Wade took a step towards her, then stopped as the other woman touched her arm. Had there been something menacing about the action, or was it just her overworked imagination running riot? After all, why should Moira Wade want to harm her? No, she was getting neurotic, seeing threats where there were none.

Lost in thought, she pushed the door open and stepped out, drawing in deep lungfuls of the clear, crisp air, then nearly choked as a soft voice said quietly, 'So I was right, after all, then, Chrissie.'

She swung round, her eyes huge in her pale face as she stared at Jackson Knight. He was leaning against the wall, arms folded across his chest, legs crossed loosely at the ankles, the very picture of relaxation—if one didn't take too close a look at his face . . . that told an entirely different story! He was about as relaxed as a panther who'd just spotted his prey, and Chrissie knew that she was the prey. She took a step backwards, moving out of the pool of light which spilled from the half-open door, so that he couldn't see the shock etched on her face. How had he known that she would sneak out this way?

He seemed to read her mind, answering her unspoken question with a grimness to his voice which made her heart flutter.

'I figured you'd make a run for it rather than face me, so that's why I asked Pete to tell you I was waiting at the front for you.'

It took one minute, a full sixty seconds, for that to sink in, but when it finally did Chrissie felt the first stirrings of anger.

'You did what?' she demanded, drawing herself up to her full height.

'You heard.'

Why, of all . . . Words failed her so that she could only stand and stare at him, shaking with anger. He'd tricked her, flushed her out like a rabbit from a trap, then calmly stood here waiting to catch her. Oh, if she were only three stone heavier and packed the punch of a boxer she would hit him for that!

She swung round, marching briskly towards the back gate, knowing that she was holding on to her temper by just the slimmest thread. He was angry too, she didn't doubt it, but right at the moment she felt her anger was equal to his and had more justification. How dared he? How dared he set a trap for her? The man was insufferable!

Across the yard, out of the gate and along the alley, temper kept her company, along with a thousand nasty things she'd like to do to him. Boil him in oil, pickle him in vinegar, stretch him out on the rack . . . there was no end to the interesting range of tortures she could think of to pay him back. Muttering to herself, she strode down the road, oblivious to the startled glances from the few people she passed as they overheard her ramblings. Evidently being hanged, drawn and quartered was something which hadn't been discussed in central London for several centuries!

She stopped at the kerb, flicked a cursory glance along the road, then shot back with a small yelp as a car drew sharply in alongside her, so close that it nearly ran over her toes. The passenger door was flung open and a dark head appeared in the open doorway.

'Get in,' he snarled.

It wasn't the nicest or politest of invitations Chrissie had ever been offered, and she ignored it, turning away to stride further down the street. Out of the corner of her eye she could see the car crawling slowly along beside her, but she took not one scrap of notice.

'For pity's sake, woman, get in, will you?' Jackson ordered grimly.

'Get lost,' she muttered in her sweetest tones. Hitching her bag on to her shoulder, she whipped round the back of the car and raced across the road, walking briskly in the direction of the taxi-rank. There was the sound of a car door being slammed, then of footsteps running, and Chrissie shot a swift glance over her shoulder before taking to her heels. The look on his face was murderous, and she had the nasty suspicion that she was the intended victim. Heart pumping, she raced down the road, dodging round a few startled pedestrians, only too aware that he was gaining on her. Her breath was coming in laboured spurts now, pain racking her chest as she tried to force more oxygen into her lungs and she made herself a silent promise that if she ever got out of this, lived long enough, then she would take up jogging to get herself fit!

'When I get hold of you I'm going to . . .'

She never actually heard what he intended, but she had a pretty good idea that she wouldn't enjoy it, and sheer terror added a spurt of speed to her tired legs. She flew round the corner, all the breath billowing from her body as she ran slap-bang into something solid. There was a moment's confusion while she and the other person righted themselves, then, pushing the dishevelled hair from her face, Chrissie stared nonplussed at the policeman, who was eyeing her grimly.

'Are you all right, miss?' he asked politely, his eyes shooting to Jackson Knight, who had just appeared round the corner and skidded to an abrupt halt.

'I . . . I . . .'

It was difficult to find enough breath to frame an answer, and Chrissie hesitated, sucking in a few deep lungfuls of air.

'It's all my fault, officer.'

With an easy confidence Jackson stepped forwards, slipping an arm round her shuddering shoulders and clamping her close to his side. 'I'm afraid we had a bit of a quarrel and Chrissie refused to let me drive her home. I . . . well, I was just trying to change her mind.' He laughed, the soft, conspiratorial laugh of one man to another over the vagaries of women, and Chrissie tried even harder to find enough

breath to speak. Of all the lying, deceitful, double-
dealing monsters, he must be the worst! If she had
her way, this nice, kind and beautifully *polite*
policeman would throw him into the darkest,
dingiest dungeon. She opened her mouth, ready to
give her edited version of the story with a few little
highlights for added interest, but he must have
realised what she intended. With a speed which
would have astounded her if she hadn't known
what he was capable of, he dipped his head,
pressing his mouth to hers in a deep, drugging kiss
which left her reeling.

'Isn't that right, darling?' he murmured softly.
He pressed her close to his side and stared at her,
his eyes filled with mockery and a ruthless
determination, and in that second Chrissie knew
she couldn't win. Oh, she could say anything, tell
any sort of tale she cared to, but when the chips
were finally down she wouldn't win; he would see
to that! Clamping her lips together, she nodded in
unwilling agreement.

'Are you quite certain, miss?' The policeman
was obviously still not fully convinced, and with a
regretful little sigh Chrissie let the rest of those
lovely little images of thumb-screws and racks fade
gently away. If she made trouble for Jackson
Knight, real trouble, then there was no knowing
how he would retaliate. It just wasn't worth it.

'Yes, officer. It's as Jack said, everything just
got out of hand, but really it's all right.'

'Well, as long as you're quite sure, then that's
fine by me. If I can just have your names and
addresses, just routine, you understand. There's no

question of me carrying this further.' He took out
his notebook, writing all the details down in a clear
and careful hand, then walked on his way, his
footsteps gradually fading into the distance.

For a few seconds they stood quite still, his arm
still draped heavily across her shoulders, then with
a quick flick Chrissie shook herself free and headed
off again down the road.

'And where do you think you're going?'

He stepped in front of her so that she was forced
to stop, his face harsh and grim in the muted light.

'Home,' she snapped. 'Why, have you any
objections?'

'None at all. I think it's an excellent idea.'

'Good, so kindly get out of my way.'

'No.'

'What do you mean, no? Get out of my way,
Jackson Knight, or I'm going to call that
policeman back.'

'And tell him what?' he asked with a mocking
patience. 'That you've changed your mind, that
you now don't know me, that I was going to
abduct you and sell you to white slave traders?
Come on, Chrissie, tell me what you're going to
say; it can't be any more fanciful than the lies
you've been telling me.'

'Lies?' she repeated, going suddenly cold. 'What
lies?'

'Lies about how much you wanted me, that you
needed time, even that you're attracted to me.
You've a damn funny way of showing it, that's all I
can say. If you're so interested in me, then explain
why you went to such lengths to avoid me tonight.

Hell, woman, last night you were willing and eager to share my bed, yet tonight you won't even let me take you home. What sort of a game are you playing, Chrissie? Because it's got me foxed.'

There was anger in his deep voice and another emotion, a very real echo of pain, and Chrissie was overwhelmed with guilt. She reached out, her hand just brushing against the dark sleeve of his suit in the lightest briefest of touches.

'Jack, I'm . . .' It was impossible to explain without admitting the real reason she had come to the club, and that she couldn't do. Her throat closed on the words and she stared silently at him, her eyes searching the strong bones of his face. If only they could have met some other time, some other place, then things might have been so different. With a sudden shattering insight she knew that she could have fallen in love with this man and he with her, but now they would never have that chance. It had never been there in the first place.

He covered her hand with his, the anger draining from his face.

'Chrissie, I still don't understand what's going on, but what the hell! Just believe me when I say that all I ever wanted to do was drive you home, no more, no less. I'm not asking for anything more than you're prepared to give me. So let's call a truce, shall we?'

He smiled at her, his eyes dark and steady, and she smiled back.

'Yes,' she said quietly, 'a truce.'

* * *

They drove in silence across the city, both absorbed
in their own thoughts, and Chrissie wondered if his
were even half as bitter as hers. Those last few
minutes had been worse than anything she could
have imagined, because she'd only just realised
how much she must be hurting him by her strange,
irrational behaviour. Somehow she'd never
imagined that the relationship she'd set out to
promote could have such far-reaching
consequences . . . for either of them. Right from
the beginning Jackson Knight had been the enemy,
and she'd been determined to use any weapon she
could against him, but nowhere had she allowed
for the fact that he might be so vulnerable. If she'd
realised that before, would she really have been
willing to do it? She didn't know. All she knew was
that it left a bitter taste in her mouth to hurt him
this way. 'Love thy enemy', so the saying went; the
trouble was, it would be just too easy to do so!

'Is this it?'

There was a note of incredulity in his voice which
pulled Chrissie's mind back from all the painful
thoughts. She stared round, realising that they
were already parked in front of her home, and she
felt her heart sink. Despite the fact that the poor
street-lighting hid a multitude of sins, the place still
looked dreadful. One of the windows of the
takeaway had been boarded up, the wooden panel
covered from top to bottom with graffiti. Used
trays and papers spilled from the overflowing waste
bin, blowing back and forth across the pavement.
Further along the street a group of vagrants
huddled together in a doorway, the sound of their

drunken laughter echoing coarsely through the night.

'Why on earth are you living here in this . . . this dump?'

He turned towards her, the pale, eerie glow from the dashboard making his harsh features even more menacing, and Chrissie shrank back a fraction, twisting the strap of her bag nervously between her fingers. He was right, of course; the place *was* a dump and she couldn't deny it, so what reason could she give for choosing to live here?

'Well . . . it was the only place I could find,' she muttered at last, not quite meeting his eyes.

He laughed, a harsh, disbelieving little laugh which sent a shiver racing down her backbone. 'Oh, come on, do you really expect me to believe that? There must be a hundred places you could have found better than this!'

She stared out of the windscreen, wondering how to answer, then finally settled on the truth, or at least a part of it.

'It's cheap, and I needed to save some money for something very important.'

'What?' he asked baldly. 'What on earth can be so important that you're willing to put yourself in danger by living here?'

'I'm in no danger,' she retorted, picking up on the bit of the question she could deal with.

'No? Well, I beg to differ. I wouldn't ask my worst enemy to live in this district. So what is it that you need so badly? Are you in debt or something? Tell me.'

He reached out, gently turning her face so that

she was forced to meet his gaze. 'Tell me,
Chrissie. Let me help you. If you need money, then
I'll give it to you, any amount, rather than have
you living here. Last night was bad enough, but
this is worse . . . knowing that you're living here in
this place without any sort of protection!'

The sheer irony of his offer was so great that
Chrissie had to fight down a burst of near-
hysterical laughter which formed on her lips. He
was offering her money, any amount that she
needed; money which would be used to send him to
prison! Pain ripped through her, so suddenly and
with such intensity that she gasped and pulled
away.

'What is it? What have I said?'

His voice was so gentle that she could feel the
tears gathering at the back of her eyes and knew
she had to get away now before she did something
foolish. She pushed open the car door and stepped
out into the cool night air.

'Chrissie?'

There were a thousand questions in his voice, but
there was no way she could answer even one of
them . . . not yet. Some time soon he would have to
know, of course, why she was here, what she was
doing and why she'd so desperately needed money,
but not now, not at this very moment. If her life
had depended on it she couldn't have told him
now, let him know exactly how deep her treachery
went. It wasn't something she was proud of.

She bent down, her eyes tracing over his puzzled
face, storing the memory of it in her mind. For that
would be all she ever had of this man . . . a few

short weeks, and a few fleeting, haunting images. She wasn't entitled to anything else.

'It's very late. I'd better go in. Thank you for the lift and I'm sorry . . . for everything.'

'Remember, Chrissie, whatever you need, just ask me.'

He leant over, his hand cupping the side of her face for the briefest moment, and she closed her eyes, adding the intimate little gesture to her growing, precious horde. Slowly she drew away and went inside, oblivious to the tears streaming down her face.

She was still determined, of course, to find the evidence she needed against him, but at what cost would it be to herself? She had the feeling it might be almost more than she could bear.

CHAPTER EIGHT

THE NEXT few days passed swiftly, falling into a steady, easy pattern, yet by the end of her first week at the club Chrissie was close to despair. Under other circumstances she would have enjoyed the routine, the pleasure of performing to an appreciative audience each night, but not now, not while she was still beset by the same massive problem of how to help Kate.

Hour after hour she worried over it, trying to work out what to do next, but no amount of planning seemed to help. Maybe it would have been easier if she'd had some idea what she was looking for, but unfortunately she hadn't. Would it be papers, records of some sort, or even the bulging plastic bags of deadly powder which seemed to abound in movies? She had no idea. All she hoped was that, if and when she did find something, she would recognise it for what it was worth. How dreadful it would be if she went through all this and then overlooked the one vital clue she needed!

She saw little of Jackson Knight through the day, but each night, without fail, he was waiting outside the club to take her home, and after that first, disastrous time she realised that no amount of protests would change his mind. It was either go with him or make a scene, and she was just too much of a coward to chance a repeat performance of that first night's fiasco!

Still, after the first few times, when she'd sat nervously next to him as he drove the powerful car across the night-darkened city, Chrissie came to realise that he didn't intend to use these journeys as an excuse to push their relationship further. He was an easy, undemanding companion on those drives, keeping the conversation to a range of impersonal topics, so that gradually she found herself able to relax in his company. However, that he was still interested in her as a woman was one thing she was intensely aware of. He had a certain way of watching her, his dark eyes following her with an expression in their depths which she couldn't have explained in words, but which some part of her understood completely! He was the enemy and she should hate him, but as the days passed it became an increasingly difficult task. It was hard to whip up hatred for someone who treated you with tenderness and caring, very hard. No, Jackson Knight was playing a waiting game; he was using time as his friend, the same time which was her enemy.

Desperate not to waste any of that precious time, Chrissie took to arriving at the club each day far earlier than she needed to. There was usually just a skeleton staff in the place when she got there, the behind-the-scenes crew who undertook the general maintenance of the building, and they seemed to accept her presence without question. She prowled around, getting an idea of the routines and layout of the huge building, yet never once did she get the chance to search the office. The door was always kept locked if Jackson wasn't there, and there was no way she could risk trying to force it open, not with Moira Wade in the next room!

Chrissie took care to avoid the woman whenever possible. There was something about her which made Chrissie feel both uncomfortable and just the tiniest bit frightened, though she couldn't have explained what it was. It wasn't that Moira treated her any differently from the other artistes, but there was something about the woman which made her feel edgy. Several times she wondered about that strange meeting she'd accidentally interrupted between Moira and Marissa Morgan, but as there was never any sign of a repeat Chrissie gradually pushed the memory to the back of her mind. She had far too many other things to worry about without that.

On the Monday of the second week Chrissie arrived at the club even earlier than usual, and hurried to her dressing-room, not wanting to cross paths with Jackson Knight along the way. He had never mentioned if he knew she came in early and, frankly, she had no desire to inform him of the fact. She was coping with their nightly meetings quite nicely, but there was no way she wanted those meetings to increase throughout the day. Too much exposure to his company could prove to be very detrimental to her peace of mind!

Soft-footed, she hurried along the quiet corridor, idly noting that the back door to the stage was standing open. Through it she could see Mac's seated outline, and something made her hesitate by the open doorway. For a couple of days now she'd been wondering what to do, how to find some more background information on Knight in case there was a clue she'd overlooked, and who better to ask than Mac?

Mac was sitting in the corner of the stage, a mug of tea in one hand and a half-smoked pipe of fragrant tobacco in the other. He looked up and smiled when he heard Chrissie approaching.

'You're early, lassie. What's the trouble, can't you sleep? Or are you meeting someone?'

It was evident from his amused tone who that someone was, and Chrissie felt her face flame with colour. For the first time she considered the fact that everyone in the place must know about Jackson driving her home each night, and wondered what interpretation they put on it! Still, her reputation, or loss of it, wasn't the major issue at stake at the moment; that was vastly unimportant when measured against Kate's problem, so with a fatalistic shrug she pushed the thought aside. If people chose to believe that she and Jackson were . . . well, whatever, then let them. They'd know soon enough that they'd been wrong!

She smiled at Mac. 'I am a bit early today, I suppose. There was some shopping I meant to do, but when I got off the bus I decided it could wait. I wasn't in the mood.'

'Well, find yourself a seat and take the weight off your feet for a bit, then. D'you want a cup of tea?'

'I'd love one, thanks.'

Mac poured a second cup of tea from a huge flask, holding it till she found a chair and sat down facing him. She blew on the hot liquid, watching little eddies of steam whirl away into the distance, wondering how to begin. She wanted to find out all she could about Jackson Knight, but how on earth could she bring the conversation round to him without being too obvious?

'Now, tell me what's on your mind.'

Easing back in his chair, Mac watched her, a gleam of understanding in his eyes, and Chrissie realised there was no point in lying. He knew she'd come to ask him about something, so why not bring it all out into the open? With a bit of luck he'd believe that her interest was purely personal and nothing else.

'I was just wondering if you could tell me anything about Jack, his family and background. Have you known him long?'

Mac nodded, the pipe clenched in his teeth.

'Mmm, over twenty years.'

'Twenty? Good heavens, I hadn't realised. Did you work for his father, then?'

She sipped at her tea, feeling surprise ripple through her. She'd had an idea that their relationship went back some way, but hadn't realised just how far. Excitement rose inside her; could this little bit of digging have struck gold first time? She would soon see.

'Yes, I worked for him and knew them all, of course: old Mr Knight, Mrs Knight and Jack's brother . . . Jonathan.'

There was something in his voice when he

mentioned Jonathan, almost an echo of what she'd heard in Jackson's, so that Chrissie was instantly fired with curiosity.

'What's he like . . . Jonathan, I mean?'

'Like . . . well, as different from Jack as can be.'

'I know they're not real brothers,' she said softly.

'He told you that?' Surprise tinged his voice when she nodded, and he stared at her hard for several seconds before glancing away, looking into the distance, as though remembering things which troubled him. When he spoke, his voice was filled with sadness.

'You're right, of course. Jack was adopted, and sometimes I've wondered if it was the worst thing which could have happened to him.'

'What do you mean?' she asked, startled.

'I mean that as soon as Jonathan came along, his mother, and Mr Knight to some extent, seemed to have no real time for Jack. Jonathan was the child she'd always wanted, you see, the beautiful, golden-haired boy she'd waited years for. I always had the feeling that she was sorry she'd not waited just that bit longer.'

'Oh, surely you can't mean that?' Suddenly Chrissie couldn't bear to accept the idea. Once again she could hear Jackson's voice, filled with pain as it had been that day in his flat, and the memory of it made her ache. She and Kate had always known they were loved, the most important part of their parents' life. What must it have been like to be denied that knowledge at an early age as Jackson Knight had been?

'I can and I do. Oh, they were always kind to him, treated him well, gave him every opportunity, but you still had the feeling that they viewed the two boys differently.'

'And Jonathan . . . how did they get on together? Were they close?'

Mac shook his head, his eyes sad. 'As you can imagine. Attitudes rub off on children very quickly, so he wasn't very old before he started taunting Jack about being adopted, about the fact they weren't really his family, and it led to trouble, believe me. I remember one time when Jack must have been about sixteen and Jonathan a couple of years younger, finding them fighting here at the back of the stage. Going at it hell for leather, they were, with Jack coming out on top, of course. He was a big-made lad even then, hard and tough despite his age. Jonathan wouldn't have stood a chance if I hadn't broken it up.'

'But why? What were they fighting about so desperately?'

'His name.'

'His name?' she echoed blankly.

'Yes, I heard Jonathan telling him that he wasn't entitled to the name Jackson, it was *his father's* name and should have been his by right. Of course, Jack just flew at him, but the damage had already been done by then, more salt added to an already festering wound.'

'How dreadful for him.' She glanced down, staring into the muddy brown liquid in the cup, feeling suddenly sick. No wonder Jackson Knight had turned into such a ruthless person, when he'd had all that to contend with at such an early age.

'After that, well, they never really got on. Oh, everything was smoothed out on the surface, but underneath you had the feeling there was a lot of bitterness on both sides. Then, when the old man died and left everything to them equally, there was talk of Jonathan trying to have the will overthrown in his favour, but nothing ever came of it. He probably knew that he'd never be able to handle the business on his own.'

'What do you mean? I thought they were equal partners?'

'On paper, yes, but even old Mr Knight knew that Jonathan wasn't capable of controlling things. Jack's the one with the business head, the one who makes the decisions and holds it all together. Without him having the controlling hand, Jonathan would have lost the lot within a couple of years. He's weak, you see, always been spoilt and pampered; better at spending money than making it. Why, when he had control of this club, things were going down the drain and fast. It's only since Jack came back and took it over that it's picked up again. It needs someone with a good business sense to control this sort of operation, and Jack's got that, I can tell you. He's a good man, Chrissie, a really good man. Take my word for it.'

He stood up, patting her shoulder, his face suddenly serious.

'Don't hurt him, Chrissie. He's had enough of that in his life.'

She stared at him, surprise sparking in her blue eyes.

'Hurt him? How on earth could I hurt him?'

'You could, lass, believe me, you could. But just remember one thing, Jack's one of the best, a good man.'

He walked away and Chrissie stared after him, feeling more confused and disturbed than ever. A good man . . . was it possible?

A good man. The phrase echoed round and round her head, sliding in and out of her thoughts for the rest of the day, as irritating and insistent as a half-remembered tune. Finally, unable to settle till she could free herself from the idea, Chrissie sat down in the interval between the two performances, a sheet of paper spread on the counter-top before her. Carefully she divided the sheet into two equal halves, then slowly and methodically wrote down all she really knew about Jackson Knight, all his vices and all his virtues. The trouble was, by the time she'd finished, the good side far outweighed the bad!

She stared at the piece of paper for several long minutes, desperately trying to make sense of it, but no matter how long she looked nothing changed: there was still more to commend him than to condemn him! A good man—was it possible that she'd been wrong all the time? Had she allowed mere circumstantial evidence to influence her far more than it should have done?

It was the first time she'd ever considered the possibility, and the strange thing was that instead of filling her with despair she felt almost overwhelmed with relief. She wanted him to be innocent more than anything.

She sat quite still, letting the idea settle gently into her mind, letting all the surges of excitement and hope smooth out so that she could view it sensibly from every angle, but it was hard to be sensible and dispassionate in the face of such a thought. If Jackson was innocent, then it would mean so much to both of them; it would mean that there was absolutely nothing in the world to stand in the way of their relationship.

The idea haunted her for the rest of the night, keeping her silent on the drive across the city. When they reached her flat, Jackson cut the engine, half turning in his seat while he studied her face. She met his gaze, her eyes tracing over his harsh, dark features, and felt the excitement rise inside her once again. If he was innocent, then there would be nothing to stop her . . . loving him, would there? It was a tantalising thought.

'You're very quiet tonight. Do you feel all right?'

His voice was low and concerned, and she felt warmed to the tips of her toes. It was good to have someone care about her this way. She smiled at him, her face soft in the dim light.

'Yes, I'm fine. Probably just tired, that's all.'

'No wonder. You haven't had a day off since you started at the club. What are you, some sort of glutton for work? Why don't you take tomorrow off? I can rearrange the schedule to cover for you.'

'Trying to get rid of me for the night?' she asked softly, her lips curved into a teasing smile.

'Far from it.' He reached out, brushing his

knuckles gently down her cheek, and instinctively she turned her face to press a kiss against his palm.

'Chrissie!' There was an ache in his voice, an ache which lit up a flare of longing deep inside her. She stared at him, her eyes issuing the invitation she couldn't put into words. With a low murmur he pulled her to him, pressing his mouth to hers and kissing her with a passion which would have frightened her before, but not now, not while this spark of hope and joy and longing burned inside her. She kissed him back, her lips clinging, moving enticingly against his, her tongue stroking over the hard barrier of his teeth before slipping inside his mouth to tangle with his, and heard him groan deep in his throat.

Almost abruptly he pulled away, raking the dark strands of hair from his forehead with a shaking hand while he stared grimly through the windscreen. Even though there were inches separating them now, she could feel the trembling shudders which racked his body and she smiled, the secret, contented smile of a woman who had just discovered her power over a man. It felt good.

'Well, I suppose I'd better go in. Thank you for the lift,' she said softly. She reached out to release the door-catch, then paused as his fingers closed firmly over her arm.

'Wait a minute, will you?' His voice was even deeper than usual, resonant with emotions which some part of her recognised, and she felt a thrill she couldn't control race through her. At this moment she'd have waited all night if he'd asked her!

'I have to go away for a few days.'

'I see. When are you going?'

'Tomorrow.'

'So soon?' she asked, startled.

'Yes, I'm afraid so. Something's cropped up which needs sorting out immediately, but I want you to promise me that you'll be sensible while I'm away, not take any foolish risks and order a taxi to collect you from the club each night.'

'You don't have to worry about me,' she said tartly. 'I'm quite capable of taking care of myself, thank you.'

He grinned, his teeth gleaming white in the dim light.

'Lady, I can't help worrying about you! You seem to attract trouble like a magnet, so just humour me, will you and promise that you'll order that taxi?'

Despite the laughter, there was genuine concern in his eyes and she softened.

'All right, I will, so don't worry, Jack. I'll be fine, really. Where are you going?'

'New York. There's some trouble brewing, and unfortunately I'm the only one who can deal with it.'

There was a grimness to his voice, but she scarcely heard it, too caught up in the shock of his answer. New York! The name slithered like ice down her spine and she looked away, terrified that he would see the expression on her face. New York was where it had all started, where Kate had been given that package of drugs; was he going there to arrange another transaction, to set up another unsuspecting courier?

The thought raced through her like an icy wind, scattering the feeling of happiness and joy, and suddenly she knew that it wasn't enough to *want* him to be innocent. She had to prove his innocence once and for all . . . or his guilt!

'We'll talk when I get back, Chrissie,' he said quietly, and she nodded, too wrapped up in the anguish of her thoughts to wonder what he meant. On leaden legs she climbed from the car, watching till the red glow of its tail-lights faded into the darkness like dying embers, then slowly walked inside, filled with a sudden dread for just what she might find.

The following day, apart from a brief, hurried visit to the local shops, Chrissie stayed in the bedsit all day . . . planning. Carefully and methodically she went through everything she knew about the club, all she'd learnt about the day-to-day routines, working out what to do down to the tiniest detail. The plan might fail, of course, but at least she would have the comfort of knowing it hadn't failed through lack of foresight, if comfort was quite the word to use!

When she went to bed her head was buzzing, whirling with facts she'd written out on paper and then committed to memory, but strangely enough she had no difficulty in falling asleep. It was as though, now she'd finally made the decision to act, she felt more settled, easier in herself than she'd been for ages. She might not like the outcome of her search, might, indeed, find nothing at all to help her, but at last she was going to do something definite.

However, next day, seated in the dressing-room, Chrissie would have given everything she owned to go back on that decision. For nearly half an hour she'd sat there, wrestling with the desire which was building inside her to put the whole thing off till later, another day, another week . . . please heaven, even another year! She was filled with fear: fear of finding nothing, and equally a fear of finding something.

If she found nothing at the club, not one tiny scrap of useful information, then how on earth could she help Kate? Yet if she did find something, evidence which implicated Jackson Knight, then how could she ever find the strength to go to the police with it and see him condemned to prison? Torn almost in two by the dilemma, she put her head in her hands and prayed for guidance.

From outside in the corridor she could hear the muted sounds of movement and voices. Life at the club was moving along its usual pattern, unaffected by the problem she was facing. It was hers alone, her decision to make, and no one else could make it for her. She sat quite still for several minutes, then slowly a feeling of acceptance crept over her and she straightened, brushing the hair from her face with hands which were slightly steadier than they'd been for the past hour. She might hate the thought of what she must do for whatever reason, but there was no way she could avoid it. Too much rested on what she found out today: two precious lifetimes depended on it.

She stood up and smoothed the skirt down over her hips, then left the room, walking swiftly to the back of the building where the security staff had their office. She flicked a glance at her watch and slowed a fraction, knowing she had to time her arrival to the minute. There could be no room in her plan for slip-ups, no matter how small.

The door to the office was closed and Chrissie hesitated, watching the second hand sweep round the dial on her watch a couple of times before rapping sharply on the wooden panels. There was a low, scraping sound of a chair being pushed back, then the door was swung open and she drew in a swift, short breath, knowing she had to be word-perfect.

'I'm sorry to bother you . . . Oh, are you having your break?' She peered past the man, staring into the small, cramped room as though surprised to see the mug of tea and opened packet of sandwiches lying on the table. During the week she'd kept a constant check on everyone's movements, and soon realised that Big Ben could be set by the regularity of the meal breaks!

'Just started, miss,' the man replied, flicking an impatient glance over his shoulder at the cooling tea. 'Did you want me for something?'

'Well, yes. I left my bag in Mr Knight's office the other night when we were . . . er . . . discussing some business . . .' She hesitated, as though suddenly embarrassed by the confession, stifling a grin as she noticed the expression which crossed his face, and knew exactly what sort of 'business' he thought they'd been discussing.

'Yes?'

'I was wondering if you could let me in to his

room to get it. My wallet and everything is in it, you see.'

'Now?' the man asked with marked reluctance.

'Please. I just have to get to the shops before they close.' She smiled at him, the sweetest, most innocent smile she could muster, then added quickly before he had time to recover, 'Look, if you're busy, why don't you just give me the key and I'll let myself in? I'll only be a couple of minutes, then I can bring it straight back to you.'

'Well . . .' Undecided, he hesitated for a second, then with a shrug said, 'Well, I suppose there's no harm in it, seeing as it's you, Miss Lane.'

He turned away and Chrissie felt her knees go weak with sudden relief and clutched hold of the door-jamb for support. It was working, phase one was actually working! Fighting down the urge to shout with joy, she made herself wait quietly till he returned, a bunch of keys in his hand.

'Here you are. You'll need both of these, the long one and the Yale.'

He separated two keys from the bunch, and Chrissie took them carefully so they got no chance to merge back with the rest. With a murmured thanks she hurried to the office and let herself in, closing the door behind her. Flicking on the overhead light, she ran to the desk then felt in her pocket, pulling out the handful of keys she'd bought yesterday and dropping them on to the blotter. As quickly as possible she sorted through them, finding two which looked almost identical to the real ones, and set them aside.

Her heart was pounding, a heavy, insistent throb

which was making her feel sick, and she took a few, slow breaths to steady herself before sliding a thumbnail between the two halves of the key-ring to force it apart. The ring was old, the two interlocking sections stubborn, but she persisted till her fingers were sore with the constant twisting and turning. With a sigh of relief she finally freed the two keys, then had to go through the whole process in reverse as she slid the substitutes into place.

When she had finished, she glanced at her watch and was surprised to find that almost ten minutes had elapsed since she'd entered the room. She would have to get the keys back to the guard, and fast. She scooped up the pile of loose keys, carefully keeping the two precious ones to the door separate, then left, wondering how she would manage to live through the next few hours. They promised to be the longest she'd ever known!

CHAPTER NINE

EVERYWHERE was still, quiet with that strange silence which fills a building after all the people have gone. Hidden in the corner of the dressing-room, crouched behind a narrow screen, Chrissie forced herself to breathe slowly and deeply to quell the rising surge of panic.

The club had closed over an hour ago when the last reveller had finally been persuaded to vacate the premises, but still she waited, waited until she could be absolutely certain the security guards were working to schedule. There were two men employed each night to guard the place, and each hour, on the hour, they worked their way through the building, checking every door and every window. The whole process took nigh on thirty minutes, so Chrissie had been informed by one unsuspecting man, who'd mistaken her interest in his duties for something entirely different! This meant that she would have just thirty minutes in between each round to make her search. It wasn't long, but it would have to do.

Suddenly, from outside in the corridor came the sound of heavy footsteps, and she tensed, huddling deeper into the shadows behind the flimsy screen, holding her breath as the door was pushed open. A beam of light swept round the room, reflecting back from the mirror so that for a second she was blinded by the glare, then the door was closed and the footsteps walked on past. Pressing a hand to her mouth, Chrissie stifled the murmur of relief which sprang to her lips. So far, so good; another five minutes and she could be on her way.

With eyes riveted to the luminous dial of her watch she waited, letting the minutes tick slowly away, then crept cautiously to the door and peered out. She paused, her ears straining against the silence for any hint of noise, any sign that the men were still around, but there was nothing. Reassured, she crept from the room, hurried along the dark corridor to the office and let herself in.

She moved quickly to the desk and switched on the lamp, angling its pale, dim beam away from the door so that no trace of light would filter out into the passage, then tried the drawers, not really surprised to find them all locked. She had expected as much, and come prepared like any good ex-Girl Guide!

Unzipping the pocket of her leather jacket, she pulled out a couple of screwdrivers and slid the blade of the smallest one into the narrow gap at the top of the drawer to lever it open. It took only a second to break the lock so that she could pull it free and search through the papers, not bothering to keep them in any sort of order. There was no way she could cover her tracks and hide what she'd done when every drawer would soon bear evidence of being forced. All that mattered now was finding what she wanted; she would worry about the consequences later.

Filled with urgency, she rifled through each

drawer in turn, but found nothing apart from the usual assortment she would have expected in any office desk. She moved to the filing cabinet, using the heavier screwdriver this time to try and lever it open, but the metal wasn't nearly as easy to force as the wood. For several precious minutes she struggled with it, perspiration beading on her forehead, till with a dull groan the lock finally broke.

She checked her watch again, calculating that she had just over ten minutes before the next security check, then swiftly and methodically worked her way through the cabinet, but once again found absolutely nothing. Every paper in every file related to legitimate club business; there was nothing about drugs, or anything which even hinted at them.

Near to despair, she crammed the papers back then switched off the lamp, crouching down behind the desk while her mind raced back and forth over the problem of what to do next. There had to be some place she'd overlooked, a hiding place she'd never thought of . . . but where?

She was getting pins and needles in her legs from her cramped position and she wriggled round to ease it, panic flaring inside her as she heard someone trying the door-handle. She froze, praying that her informant had been right when he'd told her that the guards never entered the office at night. If he'd been wrong and they tried those dummy keys . . .

'Right, it's OK here. Let's go and have a cuppa. It's been . . .'

The voice faded into the distance and, weak with
relief, Chrissie stumbled to her feet. She rubbed
her legs to ease the cramp, then flicked on the
lamp, staring round the room for inspiration.
Where should she look next? Her gaze ran slowly
round the room and her spirits sank as she caught
sight of the dull gleam of metal. Of course . . . the
safe. What better place could there be to hide
something important?

On leaden legs she crossed the room, her hands
reaching out to run lightly over the cold, hard
metal. If the evidence she needed was hidden in
there, then it was lost to her forever.

Tears sprang to her eyes and she leant forwards,
resting her forehead against the safe door, finally
realising that it was hopeless. She would never be
able to prove anything now, neither Kate's
innocence or Jackson's. The worst thing was that it
was hard to know which had become the most
important to her.

The door opened, so abruptly and with such
little warning that Chrissie was stunned into
immobility. The overhead light was flicked on, its
brightness blinding after the dim glow from the
lamp. She raised her hand, shading her eyes from
the glare as she stared at the figure standing just
inside the doorway and felt her blood turn to ice.

'But I thought you were . . .' Her voice trailed
away into silence and she just stood there, her face
pale, her eyes huge, as she stared at Jackson
Knight. Slowly and deliberately he walked into the
room, locking the door behind him, and Chrissie
felt herself begin to tremble as she saw the

expression on his face. He was looking at her with such contempt, such loathing, that she wanted to curl herself up into a tight little ball and hide away; do anything rather than have him look at her that way.

He leant back against the door, the hands thrust deep into the pockets of his trousers balled into fists, and she swallowed hard, wondering what she could say, how she could explain her presence in the room at this hour. She had the feeling it was going to be impossible.

'Jack, I . . . I . . .'

'Yes, Chrissie?' he prompted, his dark eyes skimming over her pale face with an expression in them which made her shudder. 'What are you going to tell me this time? What nice little story have you thought up for me, I wonder?' He glanced at the slim gold watch encircling his wrist, his eyes mocking as they lifted back to her face. 'Surely it's a little late to be seeking my company for another lunch date? But of course that couldn't be the reason that you're here, could it? I mean, you didn't even know I was back till I walked in, so that one's definitely out for the moment. So come on, let's hear it this time, and believe me, sweetheart, it had better be good, because I'm not in the mood for games any longer.'

The bitterness in his voice cut into her, lancing through to her heart so that she recoiled as though he'd struck her. She glanced down, desperately trying to decide what to tell him, then in a sudden flash knew that it could be nothing but the truth. Time had run out, spilling like sand from an hourglass, and there was none left for her to stall with, no explanation he would believe other than the real one. She stood up straighter, her back pressed against the wall, needing its support.

'I'm not playing games, Jack,' she said clearly. 'I came here tonight for one reason and one reason only.'

'And may I ask what it was? Or is that a rather naïve question in view of the fact I've just found you by the safe?'

She ignored the sarcasm, knowing that she couldn't allow herself to be sidetracked.

'The safe had nothing to do with it. I'm not after money, but information.'

'Information . . . what sort of information?' For a second surprise flickered across his face before he blanked it out, staring at Chrissie with open hostility.

'About the drugs,' she answered quietly, and felt her heart shudder to a halt as she saw the sudden comprehension in his eyes. Pain knifed through her so fiercely that she had to fight not to cry out. He knew about the drugs; he knew, so he must be guilty!

'And what do you know about any drugs?' he demanded harshly, walking further into the room. 'Just who are you, Chrissie? What did you really come to this club for?'

He stopped just a few feet away, staring at her as though she were a total stranger, as though they'd never shared all those tender moments just days ago. It took all her strength to answer while inside every single cell in her body was aching with a strange deep feeling of loss. Nothing could ever be the same between them again now.

'My sister has been charged with smuggling drugs into the country . . . drugs which you gave to her.'

'I gave to her?' For a second there was incredulity in his voice, then he said slowly, 'Who is your sister, Chrissie? Who is this woman I gave drugs to?'

'Kate Warren . . . Lane is my stage name,' she added quickly as she saw the confusion on his face. 'Surely you're not going to deny that you know her, are you?'

'No, I'm not going to do that,' he said quietly. 'I met her several times when she came to the club, a few months back.'

'Met her and used her to smuggle your filthy drugs,' Chrissie cried out. 'How could you do it, Jack? How could you have sunk so low as to do that to her, knowing how she felt about you?'

'And that's what you really believe, is it? That I gave her drugs to bring into the country?'

'Are you going to deny it?' she said, too filled with pain to care if she was being foolish by admitting what she suspected to him.

'Why should I deny it when you obviously have such indisputable evidence to back your accusation? And you do have evidence, I take it, Chrissie . . . good, solid evidence which will stand up in court.'

'I . . . well . . .' She licked her suddenly dry lips, glancing away from his dark, intent gaze, but he wouldn't let her off the hook so easily. He reached

out, his fingers biting into her flesh as he forced her
eyes up to meet his.

'What evidence have you got? Tell me!'

And suddenly, for the first time she was afraid,
really afraid of what he might do to her. They were
alone in the middle of the night, and she had just
admitted all she knew. What was to stop him
silencing her, whichever way he chose to? Fear
shone in her eyes, clear and bright, and with a
muttered oath he dropped his hand and moved
away, setting the width of the room between them.
When he spoke his voice was low and measured, as
though he was trying to allay all those very vivid
fears.

'Just tell me what you know, will you, Chrissie,
right from the beginning, please?'

It was the 'please' that did it, she supposed,
being so out of place in this otherwise fraught
moment. Why else should she suddenly find herself
pouring the whole tale out to him? When she had
finished there was silence in the room, a heavy,
brooding silence which she knew she couldn't
break. She'd told him everything, what she knew
and what she merely suspected; now it was up to
him to decide what must happen next. She stood
rigidly still and waited.

He lifted his hands, running his fingers through
his hair, easing the dark strands away from his
scalp as though they were suddenly too heavy to
bear. Then slowly he crossed the room and sat
down behind the desk, his eyes running over the
splintered edges of the drawers before lifting to
Chrissie, and she felt the colour flood up her face.

There was no reason why she should feel guilty about what she'd done when it had been justified, but she did.

'I see you've been through the desk. Did you find anything?'

She shook her head, filled with a sudden shame which robbed her of speech.

'No. I didn't think you would.' There was an icy sarcasm in his deep voice which flicked at her raw nerves.

'Why? Because you've hidden everything somewhere else, some place where there'll be no danger of anyone coming across it?'

'No. Because there was never anything to find in the first place.' he answered flatly.

'Do you really expect me to believe that? That you know nothing about any drugs?' she cried, her voice shaking with emotion. 'I saw your face, Jack, when I mentioned them, saw it in your eyes, so don't try and say that you knew nothing about them. It just won't work!'

'So I'm to be found guilty and convicted without a trial, am I, without a chance to give my side of the story?'

'Your side? How on earth can there be "your side" to this whole rotten business? What can you say which will make it all right?'

'Only that it wasn't me, that I didn't give your sister or anyone else drugs to bring into the country, and that before yesterday I had no idea that the club was being used as a base for drug trafficking.'

There was sincerity in his voice, a deep

conviction, and for one glorious moment Chrissie believed him. She wanted him to be innocent, wanted to believe in him so much. For a second she hugged the idea to her, then slowly the truth of it all came trickling coldly back. How could she believe him, take his word, when there was still so much which implicated him? She rounded on him, a fierce, bitter anger burning inside her for what he'd done to Kate . . . and to herself.

'And what about the letters, Jack, all those tender, loving letters which Kate wrote to Mother about how wonderful you are? And that note I found in your flat actually confirming that she would be pleased to bring a package back for you? Are you saying that they're not true, too?'

'Did your sister mention me by name in the letters, then, Chrissie?' he asked quietly, his dark eyes locked to her flushed face. 'Did she? Think about it, hard.'

'Well, yes . . .' She paused, her mind racing back, seeing the jumbling scrawl of writing. Had Kate called him Jackson, or had she, after the first time, always referred to him as J?

'Yes?' he prompted, his eyes never leaving her face, willing her to answer the question honestly, and she shook her head, her blue eyes tinged with uncertainty.

'No. She did at first, when she mentioned coming to the club, but after that she always called you J. Why, what does it mean?'

A shudder passed through his big frame and he looked away, staring down at the pale, unmarked blotter in its leather holder as though he could see a thousand images etched there which tormented him.

'Jack, what is it? Tell me.' Filled with a sudden need to understand, she stepped forwards and gripped his shoulder, her fingers biting into the warm, hard muscles. He looked up, his eyes blank in a face which seemed to be carved from granite.

'Your sister wasn't writing about me, Chrissie. I only met her a couple of times when she came to the club as a guest . . . of my brother. Jay is his nickname, the name he prefers to be called rather than Jonathan; he's always hated that. He is the one who gave Kate the drugs, Chrissie, not me, but I doubt if you'll believe me till you have absolute proof.'

He lifted the telephone receiver, and carefully dialled a string of digits; slowly she let her hand drop from his shoulder, feeling suddenly cold and empty to the very depths of her soul.

'What are you doing?' she asked hollowly.

'What you should have done right at the beginning,' he said harshly, 'and saved us both a lot of pain. I'm calling the police, so I suggest that you go back to the dressing-room and wait for them. I'm sure they'll be interested in what you have to tell them.'

It was a dismissal, there was no other word for it, and Chrissie felt a sudden shaft of fear spear through her as she saw the grim set to his features. There was no warmth in his face now when he looked at her, no hint of the tenderness and caring she'd grown used to over this past week, just an empty, chilling blankness. Had she just exchanged one nightmare for another?

The thought made her shiver as she stumbled
from the room, and her lips moved in a silent
fervent plea that once it was all over he would let
her explain why she'd done it, why she'd been
forced to deceive him that way. The prayer was
silently uttered, and she had the horrible feeling
that it might have gone unnoticed.

The police came, just two officers at first, then
more later, grim-faced men from the drug squad,
who questioned everyone. Around midday they
brought in a team of sniffer-dogs, three highly
trained labradors skilled in the art of seeking out
drugs, and within an hour several boxes were
removed from the store-room. One of the men who
worked as a storekeeper was taken away for
further questioning at the police station, along with
Moira Wade!

Chrissie was waiting outside the office to be
interviewed when she was led past, flanked on
either side by a uniformed officer, and she felt a
ripple of pure shock race through her as she saw
the woman. Obviously the drug network had
involved more people than just Jonathan Knight in
its evil web, and suddenly all she'd seen—that
whispered, furtive conversation between Moira
and Marissa Morgan—took on a deeper
importance. Just how many people were really
involved?

As Moira walked past, her pale eyes slid over
Chrissie with a hint of loathing in their depths, but
she said nothing, her coldly beautiful face

impassive as ever, and it was left to heaven to know exactly what she was thinking at that moment. Frankly, Chrissie didn't want to know; she had enough on her mind to contend with, without that.

In all, Chrissie repeated what she knew three times to three different detectives, then made a formal statement and was cautioned against leaving the country. When she left the office for the last time, the club was still buzzing with activity, with staff being interviewed in various rooms around the place. It seemed she had been right about the drugs, and about the club's involvement with them, but wrong about who was behind it all—and that was what left such a bitter taste in her mouth. It should have been her moment of triumph, the vindication of what she'd done last night, but there was no feeling of elation inside her as she walked slowly back to the dressing-room. Hour after hour she sat there, knowing she couldn't leave until she had seen Jackson Knight once again and made her peace with him . . . if he would only let her.

She'd seen him only once since their night-time confrontation, and that had been when he'd left the club to go to the police station. He had looked straight through her as though she didn't exist. That had hurt, badly, but no more than the fear which was growing inside her as the hours passed. Did the police think he was involved? Would they charge him? There was no comforting answer to the questions, nothing to quell her fears, for hadn't she believed that he was involved up until a few hours ago? There was every chance that he would appear guilty also to the cold eyes of the law.

Suddenly the thought of him being locked up, imprisoned for something he hadn't done, became too much to bear, and she put her head down on her arms and wept, harsh, bitter sobs tearing through her body as she gave in to the flood of grief she'd held in check all these long hours. Had she just found what was needed to help Kate, but in exchange destroyed the man she loved? It was a painful thought, almost as painful as finally facing up to the fact that what she did feel for him was love, not just attraction.

Finally exhausted by all that had happened, she dozed off, sleeping fitfully till someone shook her awake with a heavy hand on her shoulder. She looked up, wiping the sleep from her swollen eyes, wondering where she was for a moment, till all too quickly reality returned with a jolt. Mac was bending over her, his lined face etched with concern as he took in her dishevelled state.

'What are you still doing here, lass?' he asked gruffly. 'Everyone else left hours ago. There was no point in staying, with the police closing us down till further notice.'

She sat up, tossing the hair back from her face, and peered at her watch, taking a second to focus on the dial. Ten o'clock. Good heavens, she'd slept for hours! She swallowed, trying to find some moisture in her dry mouth.

'I . . . I must have dozed off.'

'So it seems. Come on, then, let's get you home.' He helped her gently to her feet, keeping a steadying hand under her elbow as he guided her through the deserted building. They were nearly at the front door when she stopped abruptly, turning to face him, her eyes huge and haunted.

'Jack . . . is he back? Have the police let him go yet, Mac?'

He shook his head, his face grim. 'No. I've not seen him as yet. Damned fools,' he snorted. 'Why, anyone with half a mind could see what sort of a man Jackson Knight is. There's no way he'd be involved in such a filthy business.'

Chrissie's face flamed and she looked away, wondering how much Mac knew about it all. Suddenly the need to confess what she'd done and what she'd thought was overwhelming. Maybe it would ease her guilt and soothe this dreadful, racking pain which filled her body.

'I thought he was involved, Mac,' she said quietly.

'What? You thought Jack would deal in drugs, do that just for money?' Shock echoed in his voice and she felt the tears spring to her eyes again.

'Yes,' she whispered. 'That's why I came here, to try and prove it. It's a long story, and you'll hear it all soon enough, but yes.'

'And do you still think that, Chrissie, that he could do such a thing?'

She wiped her eyes on the back of her hand, then looked steadily at him while her voice shook with emotion.

'No, not now. I know I was wrong, Mac, but the trouble is, how can I tell him? How can I make him believe that I only did what I did because I had to? I never meant to hurt him—at least, not once I got to know him. But how can I convince him of that now?' she demanded in sudden desperation.

He looked at her, his eyes sad. 'I don't know, Chrissie, I really don't. Maybe if you tell him what you've just told me, then he'll understand.'

'Do you think so?'

He shrugged. 'I don't know, lass, but all you can do is try. Now, come along, you're all in, so let's get you home. Things will all look better in the morning.'

He took her arm, but she stood her ground, refusing to move to the door.

'I'm not leaving yet, not till I've seen Jack and explained it all to him. I'll wait here till he gets back.'

'And what if he doesn't come back? What if the police keep him in custody?'

The thought was so dreadful that she shivered, wrapping her arms tightly round her body to control the icy tremor. 'Do you think they will do that?'

'I don't know. I really don't.' He looked at her with pity in his eyes as he saw the pain which contorted her tired face. Then, reaching out, he patted her shoulder. 'You stay here if it's what you want to do. I'll tell the night men you're here, so there won't be any problem. Everyone's a bit jittery at the moment.'

He walked away and Chrissie turned back, her feet dragging as she made her way to the office. The door was standing open and she walked slowly inside, flicking on the light to stare round the empty room. Was it really only a few hours since she'd last been in here with Jack and she'd realised just how wrong her suspicions had been? It must be, but suddenly those hours seemed longer than her whole lifetime.

She crossed the room, not wanting to sit at the desk waiting for his return, and pushed the door of the small side room open, then stopped dead as she spotted the man slumped on the dark leather sofa. His eyes were closed, but Chrissie knew from the grim expression etched on his face that he wasn't asleep. As though sensing her presence, he opened his eyes and looked at her, and Chrissie could have wept at the coldness in that dark look.

'What do you want?' he asked bluntly.

'I didn't know you were back,' she said inanely, flinching as she saw the bitter, cruel mockery which crossed his face.

'I see. Well, I'm sorry if my being in here has spoilt your plans. What did you intend this time? To search some more in case the police have missed anything? Here, why don't you go through the safe? That's the one place you missed last night, I believe.'

He felt in his pocket, then tossed a bunch of keys towards her. They landed at her feet with a clatter and Chrissie stared down at them through a veil of tears. She deserved such treatment, of course, and she couldn't blame him, but it hurt.

'I didn't come to search, Jack,' she said, her voice choked with emotion. 'I came to tell you how sorry I am for everything, for doubting you, for believing that you were the person behind it all.'

'And that's going to make it all fine, is it? Your

apology is going to set everything back on a nice cosy little footing between us, is it?' He laughed, a harsh, discordant note which made her shudder, and she glanced away from the disgust on his face. 'Well, lady, let me tell you that no apology you make now is going to alter things. What we had, or rather what I thought we had, is dead—and you killed it with your deceit and trickery.'

He stood up to walk past her, but she caught his arm, her fingers clinging to the smooth fabric of his jacket. She couldn't let him go like this, filled with bitterness and hatred for her. She couldn't bear it. She had to make him understand why she'd done it.

'Jack, you must listen to me. You don't understand. I had to help Kate, she's my sister. I couldn't just stand aside and let her go to prison. Can't you understand that? Can't you?'

He shook her fingers off, his own hands lifting to clamp round the curve of her shoulders, squeezing the flesh so tightly that she stifled a gasp of pain, knowing that he wasn't aware of what he was doing at that moment.

'No, Chrissie, I can't understand it. Can't understand how you could ever have believed I'd be involved in something like that. I thought I was falling in love with you—d'you know that?—and that you felt the same way about me, but how wrong could I have been? All you ever wanted from me was a scapegoat, someone to blame for your sister's misfortune. You didn't want me as a person. How you must have laughed at my blindness, when the signs were all so clear to see.'

'I didn't, Jack, I really didn't. You've got to try and see it from my side. On the one hand there was Kate, and on the other there was you. I was being torn in two by the dilemma. I wanted to believe in you, but everything was pointed against you.'

'And you just didn't know me well enough, the same as I never really knew you. There's nothing between us now, Chrissie, nothing. Maybe there never really was anything, apart from this.'

He pulled her to him and his lips closed over hers in a harsh yet strangely tender kiss which brought a flood of tears to her eyes. She clung to him, her fingers twining in the cool, silky hair at his nape, while her lips moved under his, willing him to feel all the love she had for him, but it just wasn't enough to hold him. He let her go, his eyes tracing over her face, his hand lifting to brush a knuckle over her swollen lips, and she closed her eyes, wanting to keep the memory of that touch inside her forever.

'Goodbye, Chrissie,' he whispered. 'It could have been so good between us, you know, better than anything this world could ever offer.'

'Jack!' She reached out to draw him back into her arms and let her lips work the magic on him which words couldn't, but he'd gone, walking from the room without a backward glance. And in that instant Chrissie realised that she'd just lost the most important thing she would ever have in her life.

CHAPTER TEN

IT WAS the last day of the trial and the courtroom was crowded. Chrissie looked round, her eyes moving over the faces of the people sitting quietly in the room. Some, like the barristers and reporters, had become familiar to her during the week, some were strangers. All had come together in this court, shared these few days, yet by tomorrow they would have gone their separate ways. The trial would be over and the one link which bound them together would be broken, just as the link which bound her and Jack would be broken, too.

Unbidden, her eyes moved across the room to halt unerringly on his dark head. It had been like this every day of this long week; she would just turn her head and pinpoint his position in the room at a glance, as though some sort of inner radar was trained on him. She stared at him, feeling the ache, which had become such a part of her, flare into vicious, painful life. How could she bear it? How could she bear to be so close to him and yet so far away?

As though sensing her gaze, he turned and just for an instant their eyes met, and Chrissie felt the colour drain from her face. He was looking at her as though she were a stranger, as though he'd never seen her before in his life, as though she meant nothing to him! Tears pricked at the back of her eyes and she looked down, linking her hands tightly together so that the knuckles turned white. He hated her, he must do to look at her like that, and though deep down she couldn't blame him, it still hurt. All week long he'd ignored her, looked through her, but no matter how many times it happened Chrissie knew she would never get used to it. She loved him, and every cold, flat look he shot her way was like another dart which pierced her heart.

There was a sudden, flurry of movement as the jury came back into the room, and Chrissie drew in a slow, deep breath, trying to fight against the pain. Once they had returned their verdict and the judge had passed sentence, then it would be all over and Jack would be free to walk from her life . . . forever.

Twenty minutes later it was all over, and pandemonium broke out as reporters scrambled to get to the phones to ring in their stories. The trial had turned out to be far more sensational than anyone imagined once Knights' involvement became known, but, hugging Kate, Chrissie knew that none of that mattered. It was enough that she had achieved her objective and that Kate had been set free. It helped make up just a little for all the heartache.

She drew back, stepping aside while the solicitor came up to shake Kate's hand and offer his congratulations, then moved further away as a small crowd of well-wishers gathered round her sister. Everyone seemed pleased by the verdict. Did

that include Jackson Knight? She looked round,
trying to spot his tall figure in the crowd, then
suddenly caught a glimpse of him making his way
down the aisle towards the door, and in that instant
she knew she couldn't just stand there and let him
go without making one last attempt to heal the rift
between them. She loved him, and she couldn't
bear to think that he would hate her for the rest of
his life.

She forced her way through the crowd and
hurried after him, running to keep pace with his
long strides, but he already had a head start on her.
When she reached the corridor there was no sign of
him. She ran to the outer doors and down the
steps, stumbling as her feet slipped on the wet
flags. It was raining, a light, fine drizzle which
clung to her clothes and skin, soaking her in
seconds, but she scarcely noticed as she looked
frantically up and down the street. Where had he
gone?

A car came from the car park at the back of the
court, halting at the corner to wait for a gap in the
traffic, and with a start of alarm Chrissie realised it
was Jack's. She was going to miss him. He was
going to drive away and she would never get a
chance to talk to him, to tell him how sorry she was
for what she'd done. She had to stop him! She ran
towards the car, grasping the handle to wrench the
passenger door open just as he was about to drive
off. He slammed on the brakes, skidding to a halt,
then turned on her, his face filled with fury.

'Are you mad? What the hell do you think
you're doing? You could have got hurt!'

'I've got to talk to you, Jack,' she stammered breathlessly, gripping hold of the handle as though it were a lifeline.

'There's nothing to talk about, Chrissie. We've said it all. Now, will you please let go of that door? I've a plane to catch.'

'No. Not till you listen to me. Why are you doing this, Jack? Why are you destroying everything we had?'

'Why am *I* destroying it? That's rich, really rich, coming from you. Listen here . . .'

A car horn sounded behind them, and they looked round at the queue of cars tailing back from the exit. Jack's car was blocking the traffic, and even now the other drivers were starting to look impatient at the hold-up—but it was their hard luck! They would just have to wait, because there was no way Chrissie was going to let go of this door-handle and let him drive off. She turned her back on the angry faces and bent down.

'Look, Jack, I think you've got this all wrong. You've got to . . .' The horn sounded again, longer and louder this time. With a low snarl of fury, Jack said curtly, 'For pity's sake, get in, will you? We're holding everyone up.'

Quick as a flash she slid into the car, falling back in the seat as he shot away with a squeal of tyres. She straightened, shooting a glance at his profile, and felt herself go cold at the grim set to his features. If his expression was any sort of yardstick, then she would have her work cut out to make him listen to a single word.

They drove in silence across the city, a strained,

bitter silence which seethed with tension and undercurrents, and Chrissie felt her nerves stretch to their limits. He was driving at a furious pace through the traffic, showing scant regard for other people, and she bit down a burst of slightly hysterical laughter as she realised he was likely to get them both killed before she'd had her chance to say her piece.

'Slow down, can't you, Jack . . . please?'

He shot her a brief glance, his mouth set into a grim line, then gradually eased his foot from the accelerator as he saw the pallor of her cheeks. He changed lanes, pulled into a side road, then cut the engine and turned to face her.

'Well, what's so important that you have to talk to me now?'

Cold sarcasm laced his deep voice, and Chrissie felt herself go cold at the tone. She hesitated, desperately trying to think how to begin, but her mind had gone completely blank. She stared at him, speechless and aching.

'Come on, Chrissie. I haven't got all day. As I said, I've a plane to catch in . . .' he shot a glance at his watch '. . . in just over an hour. So whatever it is, make it fast. I just haven't got the time to waste on you.'

That stung, really and truly stung! That he should consider listening to her a waste of his time! Anger sparked inside her and she turned on him, her blue eyes flashing.

'Well, Mr Knight, I'm very sorry if I'm wasting your valuable time. Please excuse me. All I wanted to do was make you understand why I'd done it, come to the club and everything, but I can see it's absolutely pointless. I'd only be wasting my breath and your ''valuable'' time, and that would never do, now, would it? Don't worry, I won't detain you any longer. I realise your business dealings are far more important than anything I have to say!'

She wrenched the car door open to get out, but he caught her arm in a rough grasp and hauled her back.

'Now, you just hold it there, lady! I didn't ask you to hijack me outside the court, did I?' He shook her when she didn't answer, his hard fingers biting into her flesh, and she glared at him, not prepared to give an inch. 'Answer me, damn you.' There was a dangerous glitter in his dark eyes, and hastily Chrissie shook her head, trying to ease the situation which seemed to be getting out of hand all of a sudden. After all, she'd come to apologise to him, not to start World War Three!

'Right, so now we've established that as a fact, then I don't think you can really blame me if I'm not too overjoyed about the delay, can you? It's important that I'm in New York by tonight to help sort out this whole bloody business, really important.'

'More important than us, Jack?' she asked softly, and watched the blankness which filled his face with a feeling of despair.

'There is no ''us'', Chrissie,' he said flatly. 'I told you that once before, so why won't you accept it?'

'Why?' she repeated, meeting his eyes, feeling the tears mist her own. 'Maybe it's because I love you too much to want to believe it, that's why.'

There was silence, a silence which seemed to stretch on forever, then he spoke, his voice so flat and cold and devoid of feeling that Chrissie flinched as she heard it.

'So you love me, do you? Since when? Since you discovered that I was innocent, that I wasn't behind all the drug trafficking, making a nice little living from all that filthy business? Well, let me tell you something, Chrissie, your love is worthless! If you'd really loved me, then by heaven you would have known that I couldn't have done such a thing; your heart would have told you. If you *really* loved me, then you would have believed that I was innocent, and wouldn't have needed hard facts and evidence to prove it to you!'

What was the use? Staring at his set face, Chrissie knew that it was hopeless. There was no way he would ever accept that she had started to believe in him way before she'd found out the truth. No way he would believe that she'd wanted to find the evidence as much to prove his innocence as Kate's. She pulled away, brushing a shaking hand over her eyes to wipe away the tears. She wouldn't cry, not now, not ever . . . not for this man who'd thrown her love back at her.

'I'll drive you home.'

'There's no need,' she answered quietly. 'I'm a big girl now, Jack; I can take care of myself. I don't need anyone to help me.'

He glanced out at the rain, a strange, fleeting indecision on his face. 'You'll get soaked, so don't be silly, love.'

'So I get soaked, I catch pneumonia and I die. What is it to you, Jack? You already said it . . . I mean nothing to you, nothing at all. So don't feel responsible for me.'

She stepped out of the car, evading his hand.

'Chrissie, don't go like . . .'

She bent down and stared at him, her eyes tracing over his face for one last time, storing the memory of it because that was all she would ever have of him now, just her memories and this racking pain in her heart.

'Goodbye, Jack,' she whispered softly. 'I hope you'll be happy. I hope you'll find everything you want from life.'

'Chrissie!'

She turned and walked slowly down the street, feeling strangely numb. As though in a dream, she heard the sound of the car being started and the roar of the engine as he drove away, but she didn't look back.

She went straight back to the bedsit, only stopping long enough to drop an envelope in the post box on the corner of the street. Just for a second, before she let it slither out of sight, she held it, feeling the hard outline of the key, the rustle of crumpled paper which was all it contained. Jack had given her this, offered her sanctuary from any storm, but when a real, true, blue-blooded gale had blown up he'd reneged on that offer. No, she had no need of this key now, no need of a link between them any more.

She spent the night packing, cramming all her props and costumes into bags and boxes with little regard for any damage she might be causing, then caught the first train she could back to Wigan. When she got home she went straight to bed and all but slept the clock round, exhausted by everything which had happened. She awoke around six the following day, still tired, yet knowing that she just couldn't sleep any longer. She got up and pulled on jeans and sweatshirt before creeping downstairs, pausing in dismay when she found Kate already in the kitchen. For one long minute they stared at each other, then Kate held out her arms and Chrissie ran across the room and hugged her. There was no need for words, both understood the other's pain: Kate had loved and been used by Jonathan Knight, and Chrissie had loved and lost Jackson. What could either say to ease that sort of torment? Yet somehow there was comfort in knowing that each understood the other.

Finally Chrissie pulled away and sat down at the table, sipping the lukewarm cup of coffee which Kate poured for her. She looked up, her eyes running compassionately over her sister's pale, strained face.

'What are you going to do now?'

'I don't know,' Kate answered. 'At this moment I feel as though I'm in some sort of limbo, half in and half out of some terrible nightmare, but I can't stay like this forever. I've got to try and make a new life for myself, but I don't know how, or even where. What about you?'

Chrissie shrugged, pushing the uncombed snarl of blonde hair from her face. 'Oh, go back to work, I suppose. I'll ring my agent later and see what he can offer . . . perhaps something abroad for a few months.'

Kate nodded, her face drawn and older than it should have been. 'It's the best thing you can do, I think. I'm sorry, Chrissie.'

'What for?'

'For getting you involved in all this. If I hadn't been so stupid, and made a full statement right at the beginning, telling the police all about Jonathan, then you . . .'

'Then I would never have met Jack,' she finished quietly. 'And though at the moment it's tearing me apart, frankly, it's the one thing I wouldn't have wanted to miss for anything. I love him, Kate, and, even if I can never see him again, it's something I don't regret.' She stood up, her emotions too raw to talk about any longer. 'I think I'll go for a walk. I could do with some peace and quiet after all the bustle and dust of London.'

She smiled at Kate, then let herself out of the back door and walked slowly up the lane, taking the path which led up to the top of Shaley Brow. The sun was still low in the sky, but she could feel the warmth of its rays striking through the fleecy softness of her sweatshirt. She took her time, but she was still breathing heavily by the time she reached the top of the steep hill. Pulling off the sweatshirt, she knotted the sleeves round her shoulders, then climbed astride the stone wall which edged the roadway, staring down the sweep of land, studying the patchwork effect of all the different greens and browns. In the distance she could see St Helens and, further on, a mere grey smudge on the skyline, the sprawling outline of Liverpool.

It was a view she'd looked at time and again over the years, one which had afforded her comfort many times as she'd grown up: would it help her now, help her to find peace and respite from this dreadful pain?

A car door slammed and footsteps broke the silence, sending a magpie which was searching for food winging into the sky. One for sorrow, she thought inconsequentially, then looked round for its mate, superstitious enough to want to see the 'two for joy', as the saying went. A man was walking down the road towards her, a tall man with dark hair which gleamed and shone in the early morning light as silkily as the magpie's feathers, and for a second the breath caught in her throat. From this distance, and with the sun casting its glare into her eyes, he looked just like Jack, but of course it couldn't be. Jack wouldn't be here; he was miles away, in America.

Racked with pain, she turned back to the view, willing the mist of tears to clear from her eyes. What sort of life would she have if she started to think every man she saw was Jack?

'Chrissie.'

He spoke her name quietly, but the shock of hearing his voice was so great that she felt the colour drain from her face. She looked round, her hand raised to shade her eyes against the glare, and felt her heart start to hammer with a dull, sickening thud as she looked into his beloved face. She couldn't speak, couldn't find the voice or the words to say anything to him. She just looked, her heart in her eyes.

'Your sister said I'd find you here,' he said softly.

'You've been to the house, then?' she asked, then chided herself for the stupidity of the question.

He nodded, climbing over the wall to sit next to her on the warm, rough stones. He was wearing dark jeans and sweater, the shadow of stubble darkening his jaw, his hair wildly dishevelled as though he had run his fingers through it time and again in that familiar way he had, but to Chrissie he looked marvellous. She could have sat there and just looked at him all day, but she had to know why he'd come, had to know if there was any real basis for the sudden flare of hope which rose inside her. She glanced away from his face, staring down at the scuffed toes of her trainers dug into the soft, springy grass.

'What do you want, Jack?' she asked at last, somehow afraid to voice the question in case the answer was one she couldn't bear to hear. 'Why have you come?'

'Because I had to see you.'

'But why now?' she demanded, a sudden bitterness welling inside her. 'You already told me that there was nothing left between us, so why do you now want to see me?'

The pain in her voice was unmistakable and she saw him flinch, his dark eyes filled with agony.

'I know, Chrissie. I'm sorry, but at the time I just couldn't help it. I know I hurt you . . . hurt myself, but I was still so cut up by it all that I just couldn't handle it. I blamed myself, you see.'

'Why, what do you mean?'

'For not realising Jonathan was up to something. Lord knows, the signs were unmistakable. He spent money like water, yet he always seemed to have more and more available. Even when I asked him where he'd got the cash to have the club refurbished and he came up with some cock-and-bull story about some investments paying out, I was willing to believe him rather than cause more trouble between us. There had been too much of that already in the past. Yes, the signs were all there: him, Moira and Marissa, all involved in that filthy racket, yet I was too blind to see them. Then, when I found out just what had been going on, and that it was the reason you'd come to the club, I really went off the rails. They'd all deceived me, played me for a fool, but it was the fact that you had done so too which really hurt. I'd fallen in love with you almost from the first moment I met you, and thought you were falling for me. Then I found out that it had all just been a ploy, that you probably didn't feel anything for me, that I was just a means to an end.'

'It wasn't like that, Jack,' she whispered, hating to hear the pain in his deep voice. 'I've got to be honest and admit that at first I did plan to do it that way, planned to use the obvious attraction you had for me to my advantage, but somehow it became impossible. I was falling in love with you, and even before I found out the truth about your brother, I desperately wanted to believe in you.

When I searched your office that night, it was as much to prove your innocence as Kate's.'

'Oh, Chrissie, you don't know how much it means to hear you say that, sweetheart.' He caught her hand, holding it gently while his thumb stroked over the back, its touch just slightly abrasive, and Chrissie had to clamp down on the sudden wild clamouring of her senses. 'You see, Chrissie, it was only when I was flying to the States that I finally came to my senses and faced the fact that you meant more to me than any amount of hurt pride and bruised feelings. I'd let you go, pushed you out of my life with such cruelty, and every mile I flew was another mile away from you. I couldn't stand it. I got to New York and booked the very next flight home.'

'Jack, you didn't!'

'I did. It caused no end of trouble over there, believe me, but frankly I couldn't give a damn. I know I'll have to go back again soon; Jonathan's disappeared, you see, the police can't find any trace of him, so it's left everything in one hell of a mess over there, but I'm not going back till I get this straightened out between us, no matter what happens.'

There was a grim determination in his face which made her smile.

'That, Mr Knight, sounds like blackmail. Either I listen to what you have to say, and probably agree to it, or you let the whole of your business go down the drain. Is that it?' She tilted her head and stared mockingly at him.

'Mmm, well, something like that, I suppose, my

love. Though perhaps I wouldn't have put it quite so bluntly.' He laughed, the tension easing from his face as he looked at her. 'How is it that you can read me so well?'

'Maybe because I love you,' she said softly.

'Do you, Chrissie? Do you really, even after the way I've treated you?' There was a hard glitter in his dark eyes, an expression which sent a curl of excitement racing through her. It stole her breath so that she could only nod mutely at him.

'Thank heaven! I love you, Chrissie. When I got back home I called at the flat and found the key and that note which you'd sent back to me. I . . . well, it almost destroyed me. I realised then that you'd needed me these past weeks, needed my love and my support to face it all, and that I'd turned away from you. You'd sought shelter and I'd not been there, but it won't happen ever again, my love, because I've finally come to my senses. I love you, Chrissie, more than I can ever tell you just in words, and I intend to be there for you, every time, if you'll let me.'

There was no doubting the sincerity in his voice, and Chrissie moved to him, putting her arms round his broad shoulders to hold him close. They stayed like that for several minutes, then slowly he turned his head, his hands moulding her body against his while his lips trailed over her face, tender, gentle kisses which lit up a flare of longing deep inside her. She moved, capturing his lips with hers, needing to feel his mouth on hers.

The kiss ran on and on, burning them up, fusing their minds and bodies and healing their souls; a swirling vortex of feeling which was drawing them deeper and deeper into its spell. They were both flushed when they drew apart, and Chrissie rested her cheek against the broad warmth of his chest, feeling safe for the first time in weeks. She'd just come home, home into the arms of the only man she would ever love, and it was a marvellous feeling.

'Will you marry me, Chrissie?' He drew back, his face serious, his dark eyes filled with tenderness, and such love that she felt her heart lift and warmth flood through her body. She smiled at him, her face alight, beautiful with happiness and joy.

'Yes, Jack, oh, yes . . . yes . . . yes!'

And suddenly knew what true magic really was!

A SPARKLING COLLECTION FOR CHRISTMAS FROM

TEMPTATION

This special Temptation Christmas pack has 4 novels all based on a single theme – the Montclair Emeralds. Enjoy and discover the exciting mystique and the secrets of these magnificent gems.

The pack features four of our most popular authors.

Fulfilment	–	Barbara Delinsky
Trust	–	Rita Clay Estrada
Joy	–	Jayne Ann Krentz
Impulse	–	Vicki Lewis Thompson

PLUS, with each pack you have a chance to enter the fabulous Temptation Emeralds competition.

Available from Boots, Martins, John Menzies, WH Smith, Woolworths and other paperback stockists.

Pub. Date
3rd November 1989

Mills & Boon

Price £5.40

ROMANCING
THE PHONE

Win the romantic holiday of a lifetime for two at the exclusive Couples Hotel in Ocho Rios on Jamaica's north coast with the Mills & Boon and British Telecom's novel competition, 'Romancing the Phone'.

This exciting competition looks at the importance the telephone call plays in romance. All you have to do is write a story or extract about a romance involving the phone which lasts approximately two minutes when read aloud.

The winner will not only receive the holiday in Jamaica, but the entry will also be heard by millions of people when it is included in a selection of extracts from a short list of entries on British Telecom's 'Romance Line'. Regional winners and runners up will receive British Telecom telephones, answer machines and Mills & Boon books.

For an entry leaflet and further details all you have to do is call 01 400 5359, or write to 'Romancing the Phone', 22 Endell Street, London WC2H 9AD.

You may be mailed with other offers as a result of this application.

FRUIT SALAD WORDSEARCH
COMPETITION!

How would you like a years supply of Mills & Boon Romances ABSOLUTELY FREE? Well, you can win them! All you have to do is complete the word puzzle below and send it in to us by Dec. 31st. 1989. The first 5 correct entries picked out of the bag after that date will win **a years supply of Mills & Boon Romances** (*ten books every month - worth £162*) What could be easier?

```
T  E  T  A  N  A  R  G  E  M  O  P
A  N  E  Y  E  P  A  R  G  A  A  E
N  E  A  R  S  P  I  M  N  N  T  A
G  N  P  R  T  L  W  E  A  D  Y  C
E  I  R  E  R  E  I  L  R  A  R  H
R  R  I  B  A  U  K  O  O  R  R  M
I  A  C  P  W  R  C  N  O  I  E  A
N  T  O  S  B  A  R  K  E  N  H  N
E  C  T  A  E  E  F  R  C  U  C  A
I  E  T  R  R  P  O  G  N  A  M  N
T  N  A  R  R  U  C  D  E  R  L  A
E  E  H  C  Y  L  L  E  M  O  N  B
```

RASPBERRY	ORANGE	LYCHEE
REDCURRANT	MANGO	CHERRY
BANANA	LEMON	KIWI
TANGERINE	APRICOT	GRAPE
STRAWBERRY	PEACH	PEAR
POMEGRANATE	MANDARIN	APPLE
BLACKCURRANT	NECTARINE	MELON

PLEASE TURN OVER FOR DETAILS ON HOW TO ENTER

HOW TO ENTER

All the words listed overleaf, below the word puzzle, are hidden in the grid. You can find them by reading the letters forward, backwards, up or down, or diagonally. When you find a word, circle it or put a line through it, the remaining letters (which you can read from left to right, from the top of the puzzle through to the bottom) will spell a secret message.

After you have filled in all the words, don't forget to fill in your name and address in the space provided and pop this page in an envelope (you don't need a stamp) and post it today. Hurry - competition ends December 31st. 1989.

Mills & Boon Competition,
FREEPOST,
P.O. Box 236,
Croydon,
Surrey. CR9 9EL

Only one entry per household

Secret Message _____

_____

Name _____

Address _____

_____

_____

_____ Postcode _____

You may be mailed as a result of entering this competition
Please tick the box if you are a Reader Service subscriber ☐

COMP7